THE PLACE OF THE LION

THE PLACE OF THE LION

by

CHARLES WILLIAMS

WILLIAM B. EERDMANS PUBLISHING COMPANY
GRAND RAPIDS, MICHIGAN

Copyright 1933 Charles Williams

Copyright 1950 Pellegrini & Cudahy

Reprinted, June 1976

ISBN: 0-8028-1222-8

PHOTOLITHOPRINTED BY EERDMANS PRINTING COMPANY
GRAND RAPIDS, MICHIGAN, UNITED STATES OF AMERICA

CONTENTS

Chapter One

THE LIONESS

From the top of the bank, behind a sparse hedge of thorn, the lioness stared at the Hertfordshire road. She moved her head from side to side, then suddenly she became rigid as if she had scented prey or enemy; she crouched lower, her body trembling, her tail swishing, but she made no sound.

Almost a mile away Quentin Sabot jumped from the gate on which he had been sitting and looked at his wrist-watch.

"I don't see much sign of this bus of yours," he said, glancing along the road.

Anthony Durrant looked in the same direction. "Shall we wander along and meet it?"

"Or go on and let it catch us up?" Quentin suggested. "After all, that's our direction."

"The chief use of the material world," Anthony said, still sitting on the gate, "is that one can, just occasionally, say that with truth. Yes, let's." He got down leisurely and yawned. "I feel I could talk better on top of a bus than on my feet just now," he went on. "How many miles have we done, should you think?"

"Twenty-three?" Quentin hazarded.

"Thereabouts," the other nodded, and stretched himself lazily. "Well, if we're going on, let's." And as they began to stroll slowly along, "Mightn't it be a good thing if everyone had to draw a map of his own mind—say, once every five years? With the chief towns marked, and the arterial roads he was constructing from one idea to another, and all the lovely and abandoned by-lanes that he never went down, because the farms they led to were all empty?"

"And arrows showing the directions he wanted to go?" Quentin asked idly.

"They'd be all over the place," Anthony sighed. "Like that light which I see bobbing about in front of me now."

"I see several," Quentin broke in. "What are they—lanterns?"

"They look like them—three—five," Anthony said. "They're moving about, so it can't be the road up or anything."

"They may be hanging the lanterns on poles," Quentin protested.

"But", Anthony answered, as they drew nearer to the shifting lanterns, "they are not. Mortality, as usual, carries its own star."

He broke off as a man from the group in front beckoned to them with something like a shout. "This is very unusual," he added. "Have I at last found someone who needs me?"

"They all seem very excited," Quentin said, and had no time for more. There were some dozen men in the group the two had reached, and Quentin and Anthony stared at it in amazement. For all the men were armed—four or five with rifles, two with pitchforks; others who carried the lanterns had heavy sticks. One of the men with rifles spoke sharply, "Didn't you hear the warning that's been sent out?"

"I'm afraid we didn't," Anthony told him. "Ought we?"

"We've sent a man to all the cross-roads this half hour or more," the other said. "Where have you come from that you didn't meet him?"

"Well, for half an hour we've been sitting on a gate waiting for a bus," Anthony explained, and was surprised to hear two or three of the men break into a short laugh, while another added sardonically, "And so you might wait." He was about to ask further when the first speaker said sharply, "The fact is there's a lioness loose somewhere round here, and we're after it."

The Lioness

"The devil there is!" Quentin exclaimed, while Anthony, more polite, said, "I see—yes. That does seem a case for warning people. But we've been resting down there and I suppose your man made straight for the cross-roads and missed us." He waited to hear more.

"It got away from a damned wild beast show over there," the other said, nodding across the darkening fields, "close by Smetham. We're putting a cordon of men and lights round all the part as quickly as we can and warning the people in the houses. Everything on the roads has been turned away—that's why you missed your bus."

"It seems quite a good reason," Anthony answered. "Was it a large lioness? Or a fierce one?"

"Fierce be damned," said another man, who possibly belonged to the show. "It was as tame as a white mouse, only some fool startled it."

"I'll make it a darn sight tamer if I get a shot at it," the first man said. "Look here, you gentlemen had better get straight ahead as fast as you can. We're going to meet some others and then beat across the fields to that wood—that's where it'll be."

"Can't we help you?" Anthony asked, looking round him. "It seems such a pity to miss the nearest thing to a lion hunt we're ever likely to find."

But the other had made up his mind. "You'll be more use at the other end," he said. "That's where we want the numbers. About a mile up that way there's the main road, and the more we've got there the better. It isn't likely to be on any road—not even this one—unless it just dashes across, so you'll be pretty safe, safer along here than you will be across the fields with us. Unless you're used to country by night."

"No," Anthony admitted, "not beyond an occasional evening like this." He looked at Quentin, who looked back with an expression of combined anxiety and amusement, murmuring, "I suppose we go on, then—as far as the main road."

"Yoicks—and so on," Anthony assented. "Good night then, unless we see you at the end. Good luck to your hunting."

"It ought to be forbidden," a man who had hitherto been silent said angrily. "What about the sheep?"

"O keep quiet," the first man snapped back, and during the half-suppressed wrangle the two friends parted from the group, and stepped out, with more speed and more excitement than before, down the road in front of them.

"What enormous fun!" Anthony said, in an unintentionally subdued voice. "What do we do if we see it?"

"Bolt," Quentin answered firmly. "I don't want to be any more thrilled than I am now. Unless it's going in the other direction."

"What a day!" Anthony said. "As a matter of fact, I expect it'd be just as likely to bolt as we should."

"It might think we were its owners," Quentin pointed out, "and come trotting or lolloping or whatever they do up to us. Do you save me by luring it after you, or do I save you?"

"O you save me, thank you," Anthony said. "These hedges are infernally low, aren't they? What I feel I should like to be in is an express train on a high viaduct."

"I hope you still think that ideas are more dangerous than material things," Quentin said. "That was what you were arguing at lunch."

Anthony pondered while glancing from side to side before he answered, "Yes, I do. All material danger is limited, whereas interior danger is unlimited. It's more dangerous for you to hate than to kill, isn't it?"

"To me or to the other fellow?" Quentin asked.

"To—I suppose one would have to say—to the world in general," Anthony suggested. "But I simply can't keep it up now. I think it's splendid of you, Quentin, but the lioness, though a less, is a more pressing danger even than your intellectual errors. Hallo, here's a gate. I suppose this is one of the houses they were talking about."

The Lioness

They stopped before it; Quentin glanced back along the road they had come, and suddenly caught Anthony by the arm, exclaiming, "There! There!"

But his friend had already seen. A long low body had slithered down the right-hand bank some couple of hundred yards away, had paused for a moment turning its head and switching its tail, and had then begun to come leaping in their direction. It might have been mere friendliness or even ignorance—the two young men did not wait to see; they were through the gate and up the short garden path in a moment. In the dark shelter of the porch they paused. Anthony's hand touched the knocker and stayed.

"Better not make a row perhaps," he said. "Besides, all the windows were dark, did you notice? If there's no one at home, hadn't we better keep quiet?"

There was no reply unless Quentin's renewed clasp of his arm could be taken for one. The straight path to the gate by which they had entered divided a broad lawn; on each side of it the grass stretched away and was lost in the shade of a row of trees which shut it off from the neighbouring fields. The moon was not high, and any movement under the trees was invisible. But the moonlight lay faintly on the lawn, the gate, and the road beyond, and it was at the road that the two young men gazed. For there, halting upon her way, was the lioness. She had paused as if she heard or felt some attraction; her head was turned towards the garden, and she was lifting her front paws restlessly. Suddenly, while they watched, she swung round facing it, threw up her head, and sent out a long howl. Anthony felt feverishly at the door behind him, but he found no latch or handle—this was something more than the ordinary cottage and was consequently more hostile to strangers. The lioness threw up her head again, began to howl, and suddenly ceased, at the same instant that another figure appeared on the lawn. From their right side came a man's form, pacing as if in a slow abstraction. His hands were clasped behind him; his

13

heavy bearded face showed no emotion; his eyes were directed in front of him, looking away towards the other side of the lawn. He moved slowly and paused between each step, but steps and pauses were co-ordinated in a rhythm of which, even at that moment of strain, the two young men were intensely aware. Indeed, as Anthony watched, his own breathing became quieter and deeper; his tightened body relaxed, and his eyes left turning excitedly towards the beast crouching in the road. In Quentin no such effect was observable, but even he remained in an attitude of attention devoted rather to the man than the beast. So the strange pattern remained until, always very slowly, the stranger came to the path down the garden, and made one of his pauses in its midst, directly between the human and the animal spectators. Anthony thought to himself, "I ought to warn him," but somehow he could not; it would have seemed bad manners to break in on the concentrated silence of that figure. Quentin dared not; looking past the man, he saw the lioness and thought in hasty excuse, "If I make no noise at all she may keep quiet."

At that moment a shout not very far away broke the silence, and at once the garden was disturbed by violent movement. The lioness as if startled made one leap over the gate, and her flying form seemed to collide with the man just as he also began to take another rhythmical step. Forms and shadows twisted and mingled for two or three seconds in the middle of the garden, a tearing human cry began and ceased as if choked into silence, a snarl broke out and died swiftly into similar stillness, and as if in answer to both sounds there came the roar of a lion—not very loud, but as if subdued by distance rather than by mildness. With that roar the shadows settled, the garden became clear. Anthony and Quentin saw before them the form of a man lying on the ground, and standing over him the shape of a full-grown and tremendous lion, its head flung back, its mouth open, its body quivering. It ceased to roar, and gathered itself back into itself. It was a lion such as the young men had never seen in any zoo or menagerie; it was gigantic and seemed to their dazed senses to be growing larger every moment. Of their presence it appeared unconscious; awful and solitary it stood, and did not at first so much as turn its head. Then, majestically, it moved; it took up the slow forward pacing in the direction which the man had been following; it passed onward, and while they still stared it entered into the dark shadow of the trees and was hidden from sight. The man's form still lay prostrate; of the lioness there was no sign.

Minutes seemed to pass; at last Anthony looked round at Quentin. "We'd better have a look at him, hadn't we?" he whispered.

"What in God's name has happened?" Quentin said. "Did you see . . . where's the . . . Anthony, what's happened?"

"We'd better have a look at him," Anthony said again, but this time as a statement, not an enquiry. He moved very cautiously nevertheless, and looked in every direction before he ventured from the shelter of the doorway. Over his shoulder he said, "But there *was* a lioness? What did you think you saw?"

"I saw a lion," Quentin stammered. "No, I didn't; I saw . . . O my God, Anthony, let's get out of it. Let's take the risk and run."

"We can't leave him like this," Anthony said. "You keep a watch while I run out and look, or drag him in here if I can. Shout if you see anything."

He dashed out to the fallen man, dropped on a knee by him, still glancing quickly round, bent over the body, peered at it, caught it, and rising tried to move it. But in a moment he desisted and ran back to his friend.

"I can't move him," he panted. "Will the door open? No. But there must be a back way. We must get him inside; you'll have to give me a hand. But I'd better find the way in first. I can't make it out; there's no wound and no bruise so far as I can see: it's the most extraordinary thing. You watch here; but don't go doing anything except shout—if you can. I won't be a second."

He slipped away before Quentin could answer—but nothing, no shout, no roar, no snarl, no human or bestial footfall, broke the silence until he returned. "I've found the door," he began; but Quentin interrupted: "Did you see anything?"

"Damn all," said Anthony. "Not a sight or a sound. No shining eyes, no—— Quentin, *did* you see a lion?"

"Yes," Quentin said nervously.

"So did I," Anthony agreed. "And did you see where the lioness went to?"

"No," Quentin said, still shooting glances over the garden.

"Are there two escaped animals then?" Anthony asked. "Well, anyhow, the thing is to get this fellow into the house. I'll take his head and you his—— O my God, what's that?"

His cry, however, was answered reassuringly. For the sound that had startled him was this time only the call of a human voice not far off, and it was answered by another still nearer. It seemed the searchers for the lioness were drawing closer. Lights, many lights, were moving across the field opposite; calls were heard on the road. Anthony turned hastily to Quentin, but before he could speak, a man had stopped at the gate and exclaimed. Anthony ran down the garden, and met him as, others gathering behind him, he came through the gate.

"Hallo, what's up here?" he said. "What—— O is it you, sir?"

He was the man with whom the friends had talked before. He went straight to the prostrate man, bent over him, felt his heart and touched him here and there; then he looked up in perplexity.

"Fainted, has he?" he said. "I thought it might—just possibly—have been this damned beast. But it can't have been; he'd have been mauled if it had touched him—and I don't suppose it would. Do you know what happened?"

"Not very well," Anthony said. "We *did* see the lioness, as it happened, in the road—and we more or less sprinted up here—and then this man, whoever he is——"

"O I know who he is," the other said. "He lives here; his name's Berringer. D'you suppose he saw the creature? But we'd better move him, hadn't we? Get him inside, I mean?"

"We were just going to," Anthony said. "This door's shut, but I've got the back one open."

"Right ho!" the other answered. "I'd better slip in and warn his housekeeper, if she's about. One or two of us will give you gentlemen a hand." He waved to the small group by the gate, and they came in, to have explained what was needed. Then their leader went quickly round the house while Anthony, Quentin, and the rest began to lift the unconscious Mr. Berringer.

It was more difficult to do so than they had expected. To begin with, they seemed unable to get the proper purchase. His body was not so much heavy as immovable—and yet not rigid. It yielded to them gently, but however they tried to slip their arms underneath they could not at first manage to lift it. Quentin and Anthony had a similar difficulty with the legs; and indeed Anthony was so startled at the resistance where he had expected a light passivity that he almost fell forward. At last, however, their combined efforts did raise him. Once lifted, he could be carried easily enough along the front of the house, but when they tried to turn the corner they found an unplaceable difficulty in doing so. It wasn't weight; it wasn't wind; it wasn't darkness; it was just that when they had all moved they seemed to be where they were before. Anthony, being in front, realised that something had gone wrong, and without being clear whether he were speaking to the body or the bearers, to himself or his friend, said sharply and commandingly: "O come *on!*" The general effort that succeeded took them round, and so at last they reached the back door, where the leader and a disturbed old woman whom Anthony assumed to be the housekeeper were waiting.

"Upstairs," she said, "to his own bedroom. Look, I'll show you. Dear, dear. O do be careful"—and so on till at last Berringer was laid on his bed, and, still under the directions of the housekeeper, undressed and got into it.

"I've telephoned to a doctor," the leader said to Anthony, who had withdrawn from the undressing process. "It's very curious: his breathing's normal; his heart seems all right. Shock, I suppose. If he saw that damned thing—— You couldn't see what happened?"

"Not very well," said Anthony. "We saw him fall, and—and —— It was a lioness that got away, wasn't it? Not a lion?"

The other looked at him suspiciously. "Of course it wasn't a lion," he said. "There's been no lion in these parts that I ever heard of, and only one lioness, and there won't be that much longer. Damned slinking brute! What d'ye mean—lion?"

"No," said Anthony, "quite. Of course, if there wasn't a lion—I mean—— O well, I mean there wasn't if there wasn't, was there?"

The face of the other darkened. "I daresay it all seems very funny to you gentlemen," he said. "A great joke, no doubt. But if that's what you think's a joke——"

"No, no," Anthony said hastily. "I wasn't joking. Only——" He gave it up; it would have sounded too silly. After all, if they were looking for a lioness and found a lion . . . well, if they were looking for the lioness *properly*, it presumably wouldn't make much difference. Besides, anyhow, it couldn't have been a lion. Not unless there were two menageries and two—— "O God, what a day!" Anthony sighed; and turned to Quentin.

"The high road, I think," he said. "And any kind of bus anywhere, don't you? We're simply in the way here. But, damn it!" he added to himself, "it *was* a lion."

Chapter Two

THE EIDOLA AND THE ANGELI

Damaris Tighe had had a bad night. The thunder had kept her awake, and she particularly needed sleep just now, in order to be quite fresh every day to cope with her thesis about *Pythagorean Influences on Abelard*. There were moments when she almost wished she had not picked anyone quite so remote as Abelard; only all the later schoolmen had been done to death by other writers, whereas Abelard seemed—so far as theses on Pythagorean Influences went —to have been left to her to do to death. But this tracing of thought between the two humanistic thinkers was a business for which she needed a particularly clear head. She had so far a list of eighteen close identifications, twenty-three cases of probable traditional views, and eighty-five less distinct relationships. And then there had been that letter to the *Journal of Classical Studies* challenging a word in a new translation of Aristotle. She had been a little nervous about sending it. After all, she was more concerned about her doctorate of philosophy, for which the thesis was meant, than for the accuracy of the translation of Aristotle, and it would be very annoying if she made enemies—not, of course, the translator—but . . . well, anyone. And on top of all that had come that crash of thunder, every now and then echoing all through the black sky. No lightning, no rain, only—at long intervals, just whenever she was going off to sleep at last—thunder, and again thunder. She had been unable to work all the morning. It looked, now, as if her afternoon would be equally wasted.

"We hear", Mrs. Rockbotham said, "that he's quite comatose."

"Dear me," Damaris said coldly. "More tea?"

"Thank you, thank you, dear," Miss Wilmot breathed. "Of course you didn't really know him *well*, did you?"

"I hardly know him at all," Damaris answered.

"Such a wonderful man," Miss Wilmot went on. "I've told you, haven't I, how—well, it was really Elise who brought me into touch—but there, the instrument doesn't matter—I mean," she added, looking hastily over at Mrs. Rockbotham, "not in a human sense. Or really not in a heavenly. All service ranks the same with God."

"The question is", Mrs. Rockbotham said severely, "what is to be done to-night?"

"To-night?" Damaris asked.

"To-night is our monthly group," Mrs. Rockbotham explained. "Mr. Berringer generally gives us an address of instruction. And with him like this——"

"It doesn't look as if he would, does it?" Damaris said, moving the sugar-tongs irritably.

"No," Miss Wilmot moaned, "no . . . no. But we can't just let it drop, it'd be too weak. I see that—Elise was telling me. Elise is *so* good at telling me. So if you would——"

"If I would what?" Damaris exclaimed, startled and surprised. What, what could she possibly have to do with these absurd creatures and their fantastic religion? She knew, from the vague gossip of the town, from which she was not altogether detached, that Mr. Berringer, who lived in that solitary house on the London Road, and took no more part in the town's activities than she did herself, was the leader of a sort of study circle or something of that kind; indeed, she remembered now that these same two ladies who had broken in on her quiet afternoon with Abelard had told her of it. But she never attended to their chatter with more than a twentieth of her mind, no more than she gave to her father's wearisome accounts of his entomological rambles. Religions and butterflies were necessary hobbies, no doubt, for some people who

knew nothing about scholarship, but they would not be of the
smallest use to Damaris Tighe, and therefore, as far as
possible, Damaris Tighe very naturally left them out of her
life. Occasionally her father's enthusiasm broke through her
defences and compelled attention; it always seemed extraordinary to Damaris that he could not in her politeness realise
her boredom. And now . . .

Mrs. Rockbotham interrupted Miss Wilmot's lengthier explanation. "You see," she said, "we meet once a month at Mr.
Berringer's, and he gives us an Instruction—very instructive it
always is—about thought-forms or something similar. But I
suppose he won't be able to this time, and none of us would
like—I mean, it might seem pushing for any of us to take his
place. But you, as an outsider. . . . And your studies are more
or less about methods of thought, I understand?"

She paused, and Damaris supposed they were.

"I thought, if you would read us something, just to keep us
in touch with—well, the *history* of it, at least, if nothing else,"
Mrs. Rockbotham ambiguously concluded, "we should all be
greatly obliged."

"But", Damaris said, "if Mr. Berringer is . . . incapacitated,
why not suspend the meeting?"

"No, I don't want to do that," Mrs. Rockbotham answered.
"It would be very awkward, anyhow, to let everybody know
before nine to-night—some of them live miles out——"

"You could telegraph," Damaris put in.

"And in the second place," Mrs. Rockbotham went on
steadily, "I don't think Mr. Berringer would like us to treat it
as if it all depended on him. He always insists that it's an
individual effort. So we must, in the circumstances, get someone else."

"But where will you hold the meeting?" Damaris asked.
She didn't want to offend Mrs. Rockbotham who, though only
a doctor's wife, had influential relations, among whom was the
owner of that literary weekly of which her cousin Anthony

The Eidola and the Angeli

Durrant was a sub-editor or something of the sort. Damaris had had an occasional article, done for the public of course, printed there already, and she was anxious to keep the gate open. Indeed it occurred to her at once that if she could only find among her various MSS. a suitable paper, she might use it both for that evening and for *The Two Camps*, which was the name of the weekly. It had originally been meant to be symbolical of the paper's effort to maintain tradition in art, politics and philosophy while allowing the expression of revolt; though Anthony insisted that it signified the division in the contributors between those who liked it living and intelligent and those who preferred it dying and scholarly, represented by himself and Damaris. He had told her that in a moment's exasperation, because she had insisted on talking of the paper instead of themselves. Anthony was always wanting to talk of themselves, which meant whether she loved him, and in what way, and how much, whereas Damaris, who disliked discussing other people's personal affairs, preferred to talk of scholarship or abstract principles such as whether and how soon *The Two Camps* would publish her essay on *Platonic Tradition at the Court of Charlemagne*. Anthony had gone off in rather a bad temper finally, saying that she had no more notion of Plato than of Charlemagne, and that her real subject was *Damaristic Tradition at the Court of Damaris*; upon which he swore he would write a long highbrow article and publish it—Damaris being, for that purpose, a forgotten queen of Trebizond overthrown by the Saracen invasion. "Nobody'll know any better," he had said, "and what you need very badly indeed is a thoroughly good Saracen invasion within the next fortnight."

Mrs. Rockbotham was explaining that she had been talking to Mr. Berringer's housekeeper on the telephone. The usual small arrangements had, of course, been made for the meeting, and the housekeeper, though a little reluctant, was under pressure compliant. Mr. Berringer was still lying quite quiet—

unconscious, Dr. Rockbotham had said. Mrs. Rockbotham and Miss Wilmot however both thought it more likely that the unconsciousness was of the nature of trance, Mr. Berringer's soul or something having gone off into the spiritual world or somewhere, probably where time didn't exist, and not realizing the inconvenient length of the period that was elapsing before its return.

"And suppose," the over-suppressed Miss Wilmot broke out, "suppose he came back *while we were there*! What he might tell us! He'd even be able to tell you something, Elise, wouldn't he?"

The whole thing sounded extremely disagreeable to Damaris. The more she thought about it, the sillier it looked. But was it worth while, if Mrs. Rockbotham chose to be silly, refusing her request, and running the risk of a hostile word dropped in that influential relative's ear?

"But what sort of thing do you want?" she asked slowly.

Mrs. Rockbotham considered. "If you could tell us something about thought-forms, now," she said. "That's what we're trying to shape—I can't go into it all—but perhaps a few remarks about . . . well, now, Plato? Mr. Berringer told us that Plato wrote a good deal about ideas, and didn't you tell me you had several studies in Plato almost done?"

Damaris thought of the Charlemagne paper, but rejected it as being too historical for this purpose. She thought of a few other titles, and suddenly—

"If it would be any good to you," she said, "I have some notes on the relation of Platonic and medieval thought—a little specialist, I'm afraid, but it would be the best I could do. If it's really any use——"

Mrs. Rockbotham sat up with a delighted smile. "How good of you, Miss Tighe," she exclaimed. "I knew you'd help us! It will be exactly right, I'm sure. I'll call for you in the car at half-past eight. And thank you so much."

She stood up and paused. "By the way," she asked, "what's your paper called?"

The Eidola and the Angeli

"*The Eidola and the Angeli*," Damaris answered. "It's just a comparison, you know; largely between the sub-Platonic philosophers on the one side and the commentators on Dionysius the Areopagite on the other, suggesting that they have a common pattern in mind. But some of the quotations are rather quaint and might attract your friends."

"I'm perfectly certain it will be delightful," Mrs. Rockbotham assured her. "*The—the Eidola.* What were they? But you'll tell us that, won't you? It's really too kind of you, Miss Tighe, and I only hope one day I shall be able to do something to show my appreciation. Good-bye till half-past eight."

Damaris, with the firm intention that Mrs. Rockbotham should have her hope fulfilled by assisting, if necessary, to print the paper in question, said good-bye, and herself took her visitors to the car. Then she went back to her study and set to work to find the lecture. When she did, it appeared even more technical than she had supposed. The main thesis of a correspondence between the development of the formative Ideas of Hellenic philosophy and the hierarchic angelicals of Christian mythology was clearly stated. But most of the quotations were in their original Greek or Latin, and Damaris was compelled to sit down and translate them at once, for fear of later hesitation about an adequate word, into bearable English. She took the opportunity to modify it here and there in case she hurt Mrs. Rockbotham's feelings, changing for example "superstitious slavery" into "credulous piety" and "emotional opportunism" into "fervent zeal." Not that Mrs. Rockbotham was likely to be worried by any insult to the schoolmen or Dionysius the Areopagite—she added a couple of sentences explaining "Areopagite"—but Damaris had only the remotest notion what these ladies supposed themselves to be doing, and even in pure scholarship it was never worth while taking risks unless you were pretty sure. The highly intellectualized readers of *The Two Camps* were almost certain to be free from any prejudice in favour of either the *eidola* or the *angeli*, but with Mr. Berringer's disciples one couldn't tell. She altered "priestly oppression" into "official influence" almost automatically, however, recalling that Anthony had told her that a certain number of clergymen took in the periodical, and after a couple of hours' work felt fairly ready. It would, at worst, give her a chance of reading her paper, which she liked doing; things sounded different when they were read aloud. At best—well, at best, one never knew; someone useful might be there. Damaris put the MS. ready and went down to dinner.

At dinner her father began talking. They sat opposite each other in the small dining-room into which two bookcases holding works on Proclus, Iamblichus, St. Anselm, and the Moorish culture in Spain had lately crept. The maid supplied them with food, and Damaris—to a less nourishing effect, but with a similar efficiency—supplied her father with conversation. He was more than usually thrilled to-day; never had he seen so many butterflies, and yet they had all escaped him.

"There was a great one on the oak at the top of the hill," he said, "and it vanished—really vanished—just as I moved. I can't think what sort it was—I couldn't recognize it; brown and gold it seemed. A lovely, lovely thing!"

He sighed and went on eating. Damaris frowned.

"Really, father," she said, "if it was as beautiful as all that I don't see how you can bear to go on eating mutton and potatoes so ordinarily."

Her father opened his eyes at her. "But what else can I do?" he said. "It *was* a lovely thing; it was glinting and glowing there. This is very good mutton," he added placidly. "I'm glad I didn't miss this too—not without catching the other."

Damaris looked at him. He was short and rather plump, and he was enjoying the mutton. Beauty! She didn't know that she hated him, and certainly she didn't know that she only hated him because he was her father. Nor did she realize that it was only when she was talking to him that the divine Plato's remarks on beauty were used by her as if they meant anything more than entries in a card-index. She had of course heard of "defence mechanisms", but not as if they were anything she could have or need or use. Nor had love and Heloise ever appeared to her as more than a side-incident of Abelard's real career. In which her judgment may have been perfectly right, but her sensations were wildly and entirely wrong.

"Plato says——" she began.

"O Plato!" answered Mr. Tighe, taking, as if rhythmically, more vegetables.

"—that", Damaris went on, ignoring the answer, "one should rise from the phenomenal to the abstract beauty, and thence to the absolute."

Mr. Tighe said he had no doubt that Plato was a very great man and could do it. "But personally", he added, "I find that mutton helps butterflies and butterflies mutton. That's why I like lunching out in the open. It was a marvel, that one on the oak. I don't see what it can have been. Brown and gold," he added thoughtfully. "It's very curious. I've looked up all my books, and I can't find anything like it. It's a pity", he added irrelevantly, "that you don't like butterflies."

Meaning to be patient, Damaris said, "But, you know, I can't take up everything."

"I thought that was what you just said Plato told you to do," her father answered. "Isn't the Absolute something like everything?"

Damaris ignored this; her father on Plato was too silly. People needed a long intellectual training to understand Plato and the Good. He would probably think that the Good was the same thing as God—like a less educated monk of the Dark Ages. Personification (which was one of her side subjects) was a snare to the unadept mind. In a rare mood of benignity, due to her hopes for her paper, she began to talk about the improvement in the maid's cooking. If time had to be wasted, it had better be wasted on neutral instead of irritating subjects, and she competently wasted it until it was time to get ready for the meeting.

As she stepped into Mrs. Rockbotham's car, she heard the thunder again—far away. She made conversation out of it.

"There's the thunder," she said. "Did it keep you awake last night?"

"It did rather," Mrs. Rockbotham said, pressing the self-starter. "I kept on expecting to see the lightning, but there wasn't a single flash."

"And not a drop of rain," Damaris agreed. "Curious. It must be summer thunder, if there is such a thing! But I do hate lying awake at night."

"Naturally—with all your brain-work," the other said. "Don't you find it very tiring?"

"O well, of course it gets rather tedious sometimes," Damaris agreed. "But it's interesting too—comparing different ways of saying things and noting the resemblances."

"Like Shakespeare, I suppose?" Mrs. Rockbotham asked, and for a moment took Damaris by surprise.

"Shakespeare?"

"Haven't they found out where he got all his lines from?" her friend said. "I remember reading an article in *Two Camps* a few weeks ago which showed that when he wrote, 'Egypt, you are dying,' he was borrowing from somebody else who said, 'England is dying, because sheep are eating men.' Marlowe or Sir Thomas More."

"Really?" Damaris asked, with a light laugh. "Of course, Shakespeare's not my subject. But what did he mean by sheep eating men?"

"It was something to do with agriculture," Mrs. Rockbotham answered. "He didn't mean it literally."

"O of course not," Damaris agreed. "But the lamb's become so symbolical, hasn't it?"

The Eidola and the Angeli

"Hasn't it?" Mrs. Rockbotham assented, and with such prolonged intellectual conversation they reached *The Joinings*, as Mr. Berringer's house was called, with some vague and forgotten reference to the cross-roads near by. The thunder crashed again, as they got out, much nearer this time, and the two ladies hurried into the house.

While Mrs. Rockbotham talked to the uncertain and uneasy housekeeper, Damaris looked at the assembled group. There were not very many members, and she did not much care for the look of any of them. Miss Wilmot was there, of course; most of the rest were different improvisations either upon her rather agitated futility or Mrs. Rockbotham's masterful efficiency. Among the sixteen or seventeen women were four men—three of whom Damaris recognized, one as a Town Councillor and director of some engineering works, one as the assistant in the central bookshop of the town, the third as the nephew of one of the managing ladies, a Mrs. Jacquelin. Mrs. Jacquelin was almost county, the sister of a local Vicar lately dead; she called herself Mrs. Roche Jacquelin on the strength of a vague connexion with the Vendean family.

"However does this Mr. Berringer interest them all at once?" Damaris thought. "What a curious collection! And I don't suppose they any of them know anything." A warm consciousness of her own acquaintance with Abelard and Pythagoras stirred in her mind, as she smiled at the Town Councillor and sat down. He came over to her.

"Well, Miss Tighe," he said briskly, "so I hear you are to be good enough to talk to us to-night. Very unfortunate, this collapse of Mr. Berringer's, isn't it?"

"Very indeed," Damaris answered. "But I'm afraid I shan't be very interesting, Mr. Foster. You see I know so little of what Mr. Berringer and you are doing."

He looked at her a little sharply. "Probably you're not very interested," he said. "But we don't really do anything, except listen. Mr. Berringer is a very remarkable man, and he generally gives us a short address on the world of principles, as one might call it."

"Principles?" Damaris asked.

"Ideas, energies, realities, whatever you like to call them," Mr. Foster answered. "The underlying things."

"Of course," Damaris said, "I know the Platonic Ideas well enough, but do you mean Mr. Berringer explains Plato?"

"Not so much Plato——" but there Mr. Foster was interrupted by Mrs. Rockbotham, who came up to Damaris.

"Are you ready, Miss Tighe?" she asked. "Yes? Then I will say something first, just to have things in order, and then I will ask you to speak. After that there may be a few questions, or a little discussion, or what not, and then we shall break up. Will you sit here? I think we may as well begin." She tapped on the table before her, and as the room grew silent proceeded to address it.

"Friends," she began, "you have all heard that our leader, Mr. Berringer—may I not say our teacher?—has passed into a state of unconsciousness. My husband, who is attending him, tells me that he is inclined to diagnose some sort of brain trouble. But perhaps we, who have profited by our teacher's lessons, may think that he is engaged upon some experiment in connexion with some of his work. We all remember how often in this very room he has urged us to work and meditate until we became accustomed to what he called ideas, the thought-forms which are moulded by us, although of course they exist in a world of (as he has so often told us) their own. Many of us can no longer walk in the simple paths of childhood's faith—perhaps I should say alas! But we have found in this new doctrine a great suggestiveness, and each in our own way have done our best to carry it out. It seemed therefore a pity to omit our monthly meeting merely because our leader is in—shall I say?—another state. We can always learn, and therefore I have asked Miss Damaris Tighe, who besides being a dear friend of mine and also known to some of you, is a deep student

29

of philosophy to speak to us tonight on a subject of mutual interest. Miss Tighe's subject is——" She looked at Damaris, who murmured "*The Eidola and the Angeli*"—"the idler and the angels——We shall all listen to her with great interest."

Damaris stood up. Her attention for the moment was centred on the fact that she was Mrs. Rockbotham's dear friend. She felt that this was a promising situation, even if it involved her wasting an evening among people who would certainly never know an *eidolon* if they met it. She moved to the table, laid down her handbag, and unfolded her manuscript. As she did so she sniffed slightly; there had seemed to come from some-where—just for the moment—an extremely unpleasant smell. She sniffed again; no, it was gone. Far away the thunder was still sounding. Mrs. Rockbotham had composed herself to listen; the remainder of the members desisted from their gentle and polite applause.

"Ladies and gentlemen," Damaris began, "as I have already said to Mrs. Rockbotham and to Mr. Foster, I fear I have only a very inadequate substitute to-night for—for what you are used to. But the cobbler, we know"—she was reading now from her manuscript—"must stick to his last, and since you have done me the honour to ask me to address you it may not be without interest for me to offer you a few remarks on a piece of research I have recently been attempting to carry out. Mr. Foster"—she looked up—"in the course of a very interesting conversation which I had with him just now"—she bowed to Mr. Foster, who bowed back—"alluded to your study of a world of principles. Now of course that has always been a very favourite subject of human study—philosophical study, if I may call it that—although no doubt some ages have been more sympathetic to it than others. Ages noted for freedom of thought, such as Athens, have been better equipped for it than less-educated times such as the early medieval. We perhaps in our age, with our increased certainty and science and learning, can appreciate all these views with sympathy if not with agreement. I, for instance"—she smiled brightly at her audience—"no longer say 'Four angels round my bed', nor am I prepared to call Plato *der grosse Pfaffe*, the great priest, as was once done."

She sniffed again; the smell had certainly recurred. In a corner Miss Wilmot moved restlessly, and then sat still. Everything was very quiet; the smell slowly faded. Damaris resumed—

"But it was that phrase which suggested to me the research with which my paper deals. You will all know that in the Middle Ages there were supposed to be various classes of angels, who were given different names—to be exact" ("and what is research if it is not exact?" she asked Mrs. Rockbotham, who nodded), "in descending order, seraphim, cherubim, thrones, dominations, virtues, princes, powers, archangels, angels. Now these hierarchized celsitudes are but the last traces in a less philosophical age of the ideas which Plato taught his disciples existed in the spiritual world. We may not believe in them as actually existent—either ideas or angels—but here we have what I may call two selected patterns of thought. Let us examine the likenesses between them; though first I should like to say a word on what the path was by which imaginations of the Greek seer became the white-robed beings invoked by the credulous piety of Christian Europe, and familiar to us in many paintings.

"Alexandria——"

As if the word had touched her poignantly Miss Wilmot shrieked and sprang to her feet. "Look, look," she screamed. "On the floor!"

Damaris stared at the floor, and saw nothing unusual. But she had no long time to look. Miss Wilmot was crouching back in her corner, still shrieking. All the room was in disorder. Mrs. Rockbotham was on her feet and alternately saying fiercely—"Miss Wilmot! Dora! be quiet!" and asking generally "Will someone take her out?"

"The snake!" Dora Wilmot shrieked. "The crowned snake!"

So highly convinced and convincing did the words sound that there was a general stir of something remarkably like terror. Damaris herself was startled. Mr. Foster was standing close to her, and she saw him look searchingly round the room, as she had felt herself doing. Their eyes met, and she said smiling, "Do you see anything like a crowned snake, Mr. Foster?"

"No, Miss Tighe," Mr. Foster said. "But I can't perhaps see what she sees. Dora Wilmot may be a fool, but she's a sincere fool."

"Can't you get her away, Mr. Foster?" Mrs. Rockbotham asked. "Perhaps you and I together—shall we try?"

"By all means," Mr. Foster answered. "By all means let us try."

The two of them crossed to the corner where Miss Wilmot, now risen from crouching and standing upright and flat against the wall, had with that change of position left off screaming and was now gently moaning. Her eyes were looking past Damaris to where at that end of the room there was an empty space before the French windows.

Mrs. Rockbotham took her friend's arm. "Dora, what do you mean by it?" she said firmly. "You'd better go home."

"O Elise," Dora Wilmot said, without moving her eyes, "can't you see? look, look, there it goes!" Her voice dropped to a whisper, and again she uttered in a tone of terror and awe: "the snake! the crowned snake!"

Mr. Foster took her other hand. "What is it doing?" he asked in a low voice. "We can't all see clearly. Tell me, quietly, what is it doing?"

"It is gliding about, slowly," Miss Wilmot said. "It's looking round. Look, how it's moving its head! It's so *huge!*"

In the silence that had fallen on the room Damaris heard the colloquy. She was very angry. If these hysterical nincompoops were to be allowed to interrupt her careful analysis of Platonic and medieval learning, she wished she had never taken all that trouble about her paper. "Crowned snake indeed," she thought. "The shrieking imbecile! Are they never going to get her away?"

"Yes, O yes!" Miss Wilmot moaned. "I daren't stop. I—no, no, I daren't stop!"

"Come then," Mr. Foster said. "This way; the door's just here by you. But you're not afraid of it, are you?"

"Yes . . . no . . . yes, I am, I am," Dora moaned again. "It's too—O let's get away."

Mrs. Rockbotham released the arm she held. Mr. Foster, one hand still holding Miss Wilmot's, felt with his other for the door-handle. Damaris was watching them, as were all the rest—without her indignation—when suddenly everyone sprang into movement. There was a rush for the door; screams, not Miss Wilmot's, sounded. Damaris herself, startled and galvanized, moved hastily forward, colliding with a heavy mass in flight which turned out to be Mrs. Roche Jacquelin. For from behind her, away towards those open windows, soft but distinct, there had come, or seemed to come, the sound of a gentle and prolonged hiss. Terror caught them all; following Mr. Foster and his charge, they squeezed and thrust themselves through the door. Only Damaris, after that first instinctive movement, restrained herself; only Mrs. Rockbotham, a little conscious of dignity still, allowed herself to be last. After the panic those two went, drawn by it but resisting its infection. The room lay empty and still in the electric light, unless indeed there passed across it then a dim form, which, heavy, long, and coiling, issued slowly through the open window into a silent world where for that moment nothing but the remote thunder was heard.

Chapter Three

THE COMING OF THE BUTTERFLIES

Anthony shook his head reproachfully at Damaris over the coffee cups.

"You know," he said, "if I were a sub-editor on anything but a distinguished literary paper, I should say you were playing with me—playing fast and loose."

"Don't be absurd, Anthony," Damaris answered.

"I come and I go," Anthony went on, "and you will and you won't. And——"

"But I've told you what I will," Damaris said. "I'm not sure whether you and I could make a success of marriage. And anyhow I won't think about anything of the kind till I've got my degree. Of course, if you think more of yourself than of me——"

"Well, naturally I do," Anthony interrupted. "Who doesn't? Am I a saint or an Alexandrian gnostic? Don't let's ask rhetorical questions, darling."

"I'm not doing anything of the kind," Damaris said, coldly. "But you must be willing to wait a little while. I'm not sure of myself."

"It's all you are sure of—besides Abelard," Anthony said. "And with you, that covers everything else."

"I think you're rather unkind," Damaris answered. "We both like each other——"

"Dearest, I don't like you a bit," Anthony interrupted again. "I think you're a very detestable, selfish pig and prig. But I'm often wildly in love with you, and so I see you're not. But I'm sure your only chance of salvation is to marry me."

34

The Coming of the Butterflies

"Really, Anthony!" Damaris got up from the table. "Chance of salvation, indeed! And from what, I should like to know?"

"Nobody else", Anthony went on, "sees you as you are. Nobody else will give you such a difficult and unpleasant time as I do. You'll never be comfortable, but you may be glorious. You'd better think over it."

Damaris said nothing. Anthony, it was clear, was in one of his difficult fits; and if it hadn't been for *The Two Camps*——. There was a short silence, then he too stood up.

"Well," he said, "you've not been eaten by the lion, and I've been mauled by the lioness. I think I will now go and look for the other lioness."

Damaris half-turned and smiled at him over her shoulder. "Do I maul you?" she asked. "Am I a pig and a prig—just because I like my work?"

Anthony gazed at her solemnly. "You are the Sherbet of Allah, and the gold cup he drinks it out of," he said slowly. "You are the Night of Repose and the Day of Illumination. You are, incidentally, a night with a good deal of rain and a day with a nasty cold wind. But that may be merely Allah's little game."

"I hate being bad friends with you," Damaris said, with perfect truth, and gave him her hand.

"But I", said Anthony, as he kissed it, "hate being good friends. Besides, I don't think you could be."

"What, a bad friend?"

"No, a good one," Anthony said, almost sadly. "It's all right, I suppose; it isn't your fault—or at least it wasn't. You were made like it by the Invisibles that created you."

"Why are you always so rude to me, Anthony?" she asked, as wistfully as she thought desirable, but keeping rather on the side of intellectual curiosity than of hurt tenderness.

"I shall be ruder to the other lioness," he said. "It's only a way of saying, 'Hear thou my protestation'—and making quite sure you do."

"But what do you mean—look for the lioness?" Damaris asked. "You're not anxious to find it, are you?"

Anthony smiled at her. "Well, you want to work," he said, "and I could do with a walk. And so, one way and another——" He drew her a little closer to him, but as she moved they both suddenly paused. There struck momentarily into their nostrils—what Damaris recognized and Anthony didn't —a waft of the horrible stench that had assailed her on the previous night in the house where Mr. Berringer lay insensible. It was gone in a second or two, but to each of them it was obvious that the other had smelt it.

"My God!" Anthony said involuntarily, as Damaris shuddered and threw back her head. "What's the matter with your drains?"

"Nothing," Damaris said sharply. "But what—did you smell something?"

"*Smell*," Anthony exclaimed. "It was like a corpse walking. Or a beast out of a jungle. What on earth is it?" He sniffed experimentally. "No, it's gone. It *must* be your drains."

"It isn't our drains," Damaris said crossly. "I smelt it at that house last night, only not nearly so strongly; but how it got here——! It can't be the frock—I wasn't wearing it. How horrible!"

They were standing staring at one another, and she shook herself abruptly, then, recovering her normal remoteness, "I shall go and have a bath," she said. It occurred to her that the smell might be, in some way, clinging to her hair, but she wasn't going to admit to Anthony that anything about her could be even remotely undesirable, so she ended—"It makes one feel to need it."

"It does," Anthony said. "I suppose the lioness——"

"In a town—unseen? My dear Anthony!"

He looked out of the window at the street and the houses opposite. People were going by; a car stopped; a policeman came into sight. "Why, no," he said, "I suppose not. Well—it's

36

funny. Anyhow, I'm off now. Goodbye, and do think about salvation."

"Goodbye," she said. "Thank you for coming, and if I ever seem to need it I will. But I've read a good deal about salvation, you know, in all those tiresome texts of one sort and another."

"Yes," Anthony answered, as they came into the hall. "Reading isn't perhaps—the texts are not quite the ritual. Send for me if you want me at any time. I love you. Goodbye."

He came into the street, frowning, though at what he hardly knew. It was usually at Damaris. He was on these visits provoked by her ignorance of his intelligence; he was provoked even more deeply by her ignorance of his authority over himself. Walking slowly away, he had often asked himself whether—in that momentary opportunity of choice which recurrently presented itself to his mind—he ought not so to exercise it as to turn his preoccupation from her. Only he did not see what good would be done, assuming that he could and did. She thought herself so intellectual and scholarly and capable—and so she was. But she was also an absurd, tender, uncertain little thing, with childish faults of greediness and conceit, and Anthony felt strongly that no one except himself was likely to recognize the childishness. They all took her at her own valuation, and some liked her and some disliked her. But to him she so often seemed like a child with its face against the window-pane, looking for the rain to stop so that the desired satisfaction might arrive. Her learning, her articles, her doctorate—and the picnic would be ended, and she would be fortunate if she were not, like most people, tired and cross and unhappy before the end of the day. Perhaps then he could be really of use—good. And if he chose to do it, it was his business. So on the whole he thought that Authority—which meant his decision—was on the side of going on. Only then Authority must control his own mental and physical irritations a little better. Self-reverence was absurd, self-knowledge was hopeless; self-control—perhaps a little more. . . .

He switched his thoughts on to another track. For the past forty hours Quentin and he had discussed, whenever they had been together in the rooms they shared in Notting Hill, little but the mysterious business of Tuesday night. They had gone over every incident without result. Lionesses didn't change into lions; nor did lions appear on small country lawns. But then what had happened? Had they been under some sort of hypnotism? Who was this very odd Mr. Berringer, in whose garden lions leapt out of nothing and who (he had gathered from Damaris) went off into reputed trances? Quentin had been almost terrified ever since, poor fellow! He seemed to think one or other of the beasts was on his track. And now this tale of a woman's hysterics and a crowned snake; and this horrible smell that had penetrated into the Tighes' dining-room. Of course, that a woman should be upset—of course, that the drains should go wrong—— But it was the other thing that held his concern. He had felt, it seemed to him now, a curious fascination as he gazed at that immense and royal beast—not terror at all; he had for an instant been almost inclined to go out and meet it. But what about the lioness? Well—there was no getting away from it—the lioness had just vanished, whatever people with guns might say. Vanished.

Revolving alternately the possibility of a lioness being changed into a lion, and of Damaris being converted to humility and love, he walked on along the road into which he and Quentin had turned two days earlier, until he had passed the cross-roads and drawn near to the house of the meeting. Why he was going here he wasn't a bit clear, unless—which seemed silly—it were on the chance of seeing the lion again. His mind recalled it as it had stood there: majestic, awful, complete, gazing directly in front of it, with august eyes. And huge—huger than any lion Anthony had ever seen or dreamt of. The lions he had seen had been a kind of unsatisfactory yellow, but this in spite of the moonlight had been more like gold, with a terrific and ruddy mane covering its neck and shoulders. A mythical, an archetypal lion.

By the gate, when he reached the house, were two men; a car stood by. One of the men was Mr. Tighe, complete with the paraphernalia of active entomology; the other was a stranger who, as Anthony came up, got into his car and drove off. Mr. Tighe exclaimed with pleasure as he recognized Anthony, and shook hands.

"And what brings you down this way?" he asked happily.

"O—things!" Anthony answered. He suspected that Mr. Tighe would take this to mean Damaris, but he didn't mind that. Mr. Tighe and he had, though they never spoke of it, a common experience. Damaris treated her father's hobby and her lover's heart with equal firmness, and made her profit out of both of them. "Lionesses don't keep you from your butterflies?"

"They seem to think it's gone farther away. I don't suppose it would hurt me," Mr. Tighe said. "And even if it did—when I think of the number of butterflies I've caught—I should feel it was only fair. Tit for tat, you know. The brutes—if you can call a butterfly a brute—getting a little of their own back. They deserve to."

"In England perhaps," Anthony allowed, "but do you think altogether?" He liked to talk to Mr. Tighe, and was content for a few minutes to lean on the gate and chat. "Haven't the animals had it a good deal their own way on the earth?"

The other shook his head. "Think of the great monsters," he said. "The mammoth and the plesiosaurus and the sabre-toothed tiger. Think of what butterflies must have been once, what they are now in the jungles. But they will pass with the jungles. Man must conquer, but I should feel a sympathy with the last campaign of the brutes."

"I see—yes," Anthony said. "I hadn't thought of it like that. Do you think the animals will die out?"

"Perhaps," Tighe said. "When we don't want them for transport—or for food—what will be left to them but the zoos?

The birds and the moths, I suppose, will be the last to go. When all the trees are cut down."

"But", objected Anthony, "all the trees won't be cut down. What about forestry and irrigation and so on?"

"O," Mr. Tighe said, "there may be tame forests, with artificially induced butterflies. That will be only a larger kind of zoo. The real thing will have passed."

"And even if they do," Anthony asked, "will man have lost anything very desirable? What after all has a lioness to show us that we cannot know without her? Isn't all real strength to be found within us?"

"It may be," Mr. Tighe answered. "It may be that man will have other enemies and other joys—better perhaps. But the older ones were very lovely."

They ceased speaking, and remained leaning on the gate in silence. Anthony's eyes, passing over the garden, remained fixed where, two nights before, he had thought he saw the form of a lion. It seemed to him now, as he gazed, that a change had taken place. The smooth grass of the lawn was far less green than it had been, and the flowers in the beds by the house walls, on either side of the door, were either dying or already withered. Certainly he had not been in a state to notice much, but there had been left with him a general impression of growth and colour. Neither growth nor colour were now there: all seemed parched. Of course, it was hot, but still. . . .

There was a sudden upward sweep of green and orange through the air in front of him: he blinked and moved. As he recovered himself he saw, with startled amazement, that in the centre of the garden, almost directly above the place where he had seen the lion, there floated a butterfly. But—a butterfly! It was a terrific, colossal butterfly, it looked as if it were two feet or more across from wing-tip to wing-tip. It was tinted and coloured with every conceivable brightness; green and orange predominating. It was moving upward in spiral flutterings, upward to a certain point, from which it seemed directly to fall close to the ground, then again it began its upward sweep, and again hovered and fell. Of the two men it seemed to be unaware; lovely and self-sufficient it went on with its complex manœuvres in the air. Anthony, after a few astonished minutes, took his eyes from it, and looked about him, first with a general gaze at all his surroundings, then more particularly at Mr. Tighe. The little man was pressed against the gate, his mouth slightly open, his eyes full of plenary adoration, his whole being concentrated on the perfect symbol of his daily concern. Anthony saw that it was no good speaking to him. He looked back at the marvel in time to see, from somewhere above his own head, another brilliancy—but much smaller—flash through the air, almost as if some ordinary butterfly had hurled itself towards its more gigantic image. And another followed it, and another, and as Anthony, now thoroughly roused, sprang up and aside, to see the better, he beheld the air full of them. Those of which he had caught sight were but the scattered first comers of a streaming host. Away across the fields they came, here in thick masses, there in thinner lines, white and yellow, green and red, purple and blue and dusky black. They were sweeping round, in great curving flights; mass following after mass, he saw them driving forward from far away, but not directly, taking wide distances in their sweep, now on one side, now on another, but always and all of them speeding forward towards the gate and the garden beyond. Even as a sudden new rush of aerial loveliness reached that border he turned his head, and saw a cloud of them hanging high above the butterfly of the garden, which rushed up towards them, and then, carrying a whirl of lesser iridescent fragilities with it, precipitated itself down its steep descent; and as it swept, and hovered, and again mounted, silent and unresting, it was alone. Alone it went soaring up, alone to meet another congregation of its hastening visitors, and then again multitudinously fell, and hovered; and again alone went upward to the tryst.

The Coming of the Butterflies

Bewildered and distracted, Anthony caught his companion's arm. Mr. Tighe was by now almost hanging to the gate, his hands clutching frenziedly to the topmost bar, his jaws working. Noises were coming from his mouth; the sweat stood in the creases of his face. He gobbled at the soft-glowing vision; he uttered little cries and pressed himself against the bars; his knees were wedged between them, and his feet drawn from the ground in the intensity of his apprehension. And over him faster and thicker the great incursion passed, and the air over the garden was filled with butterflies, streaming, rising, sinking, hovering, towards their centre, and farther now than Anthony's eyes could see the single host of all that visitation rose and fell, only whenever he saw it towards the ground, it turned upwards in a solitary magnificence and whenever, having risen, it dropped again, it went encircled by innumerable tiny bodies and wings.

Credulous, breathless, he gazed, until after times unreckoned had passed, there seemed to be a stay. Lesser grew the clouds above; smaller the flights that joined them. Now there were but a score and now but twelve or ten—now only three tardy dancers waited above for the flight of their vision; and as again it rose, but one—coming faster than all the rest, reaching its strange assignation as it were at the last permitted moment, joining its summoning lord as it rose for the last time, and falling with it; and then the great butterfly of the garden floated idly in the empty air, and the whole army of others had altogether vanished from sight, and from knowledge. It also after a short while rose, curvetting, passed upwards towards the roof of the house, settled there for a moment, a glowing splendour upon the red tiles, swept beyond it, and disappeared.

Anthony moved and blinked, took a step or two away, looked round him, blinked again, and turned back to Mr. Tighe. He was about to speak, but, seeing the other man's face, he paused abruptly. The tears were running down it; as his hands released the bars Anthony saw that he was trembling all over; he stumbled and could not get his footing upon the road. Anthony caught and steadied him.

"O glory, glory," Mr. Tighe said. "O glory everlasting!"

Anthony said nothing; he couldn't begin to think of anything to say. Mr. Tighe, apparently collecting himself, went an unconscious pace or two on, and stopped.

"O that I should see it!" he said again. "O glory be to it!" He wiped away his tears with his knuckles, and looked back at the garden. "O the blessed sight," he went on. "And I saw it. O what have I done to deserve it?"

"What . . . what do you think . . ." Anthony desisted, his companion was so obviously not listening. Mr. Tighe in a little run went back to the gate, and bobbed half across it, making inarticulate murmurs. These gradually ceased, and, pulling himself upright, he remained for a few minutes gazing devoutly at the garden. Then with a deep sigh he turned to face Anthony.

"Well," he said normally, "I suppose I ought to be getting back. Which way are you going?"

"I think I'll come back with you," Anthony answered. "I don't feel capable of walking on as I meant to. Besides," he added diffidently, "I should be very much obliged to you if you could explain this."

Mr. Tighe picked up his net, which was lying on the road, patted himself here and there, gave a final beatific glance at the garden, put his cap straight, and began to walk on. "Well, as to explaining," he said doubtfully, "I couldn't tell you anything you don't know."

"It seems to me someone ought to be able to tell me quite a lot I don't know," Anthony murmured, but Mr. Tighe only answered, "I always knew they were real, but to think I should see them."

"See them?" Anthony ventured.

"See the kingdom and the power and the glory," Mr. Tighe answered. "O what a day this has been!" He looked

43

round at the tall young man pacing by his side. "You know, I did believe it."

"I am quite sure you did," Anthony answered gravely. "I wish you'd believe as well, Mr. Tighe, that I only want to understand, if I can, what it seems to you happened over there. Because I can't think that I really saw a lot of butter-flies vanishing entirely. But that was what it looked like."

"Did it now?" Mr. Tighe said. "Well, but the thing is—— You see, it proved they were real, and I always believed that. Damaris doesn't."

"No," Anthony agreed, with a doubtful smile, "Damaris probably doesn't—whatever you mean by real. But she will."

"Will she?" Mr. Tighe replied, with an unexpected scepticism. "Well perhaps . . . one of these days."

"If there is any reality," Anthony said vigorously, "then Damaris shall jolly well know it, if I have anything to do with her. Wouldn't she like to hear me say so, bless her for a self-absorbed little table-maker. But about this reality of yours——"

Mr. Tighe seemed to make an effort or two at phrases, but presently he gave it up. "It's no good," he said apologetically; "if you didn't see it, it's no good."

"I saw clouds and clouds of butterflies, or I thought I did, all just disappearing," Anthony repeated. "And that monstrous one in the middle."

"Ah, don't call it that," the older man protested. "That . . . O that!"

He abandoned speech in a subdued rapture; and in a despair at making anything of anything Anthony followed his example. Something very queer seemed to be going on at that house in the country road. The lion—and the butterflies—and the tale Damaris had, with apparent laughter and real indignation, told him of Miss Wilmot and a crowned snake—and the stench she had known there—and Mr. Berringer's curious collapse. . . .

The Coming of the Butterflies

"How is this Mr. Berringer?" he asked suddenly.

"That was Dr. Rockbotham you saw with me," Tighe answered. "He said there was no change. But he didn't give me a very clear idea of what was wrong. He said something about an intermittent suspension of the conscious vital faculties, but it was all very obscure."

"Well," Anthony said, as they reached the road leading to the station, "I don't think I'll come back with you. A little silent meditation, I fancy, is what I need." He looked seriously at his companion. "And you?"

"I am going to look at my butterflies, and recollect everything we saw," Mr. Tighe answered. "It's the only thing I can do. I was always certain they were true."

He shook hands and walked quickly away. Anthony stood and watched him. "And what in God's own most holy name", he asked himself, "does the man mean by that? But he's believed it all along anyhow. O darling, O Damaris my dear, whatever will you do if one day you find out that Abelard was true?"

Half sadly, he shook his head after Mr. Tighe's retreating figure, and then wandered off towards the station.

Chapter Four

THE TWO CAMPS

But that evening Anthony, lying in a large chair, contemplated Quentin with almost equal bewilderment. For he had never known his friend so disturbed, so almost hysterical with—but what it was with Anthony could not understand. The window of their common sitting-room looked out westward over the houses of Shepherd's Bush, and every now and then Quentin would look at it, with such anxiety and distress that Anthony found himself expecting he knew not what to enter—a butterfly or a lion perhaps, he thought absurdly. A winged lion—Venice—Saint Mark. Perhaps Saint Mark was riding about over London on a winged lion, though why Quentin should be so worried about Saint Mark he couldn't think. The lion they had seen (if they had) wasn't winged, or hadn't seemed to be. Somewhere Anthony vaguely remembered to have seen a picture of people riding on winged lions—some Bible illustration, he thought, Daniel or the Apocalypse. He had forgotten what they were doing, but he had a general vague memory of swords and terrible faces, and a general vague idea that it all had something to do with wasting the earth.

Quentin went back to the window, and, standing by one corner, looked out. Anthony picked up a box of matches, and, opening it by accident upside down, dropped a number on the floor. Quentin leapt round.

"What was that?" he asked sharply.

"Me," said Anthony. "Sorry; it was pure lazy stupidity."

"Sorry," said Quentin in turn. "I seem all on edge tonight."

"I thought you weren't very happy," Anthony said affectionately. "What's . . . if there's anything, I mean, that I can do. . . ."

Quentin came back and dropped into a chair. "I don't know what's got me," he said. "It all began with that lioness. Silly of me to feel it like that. But a lioness *is* a bit unusual. It *was* a lioness, wasn't it?" he asked anxiously.

They had been over this before. And again Anthony, with the best will in the world to say the right thing, found himself hampered by an austere intellectual sincerity. It probably had been, it must have been, a lioness. But it was not the lioness that he had chiefly seen, nor was it a lioness which he had, on the night before, dreamed he had seen stalking over hills and hills and hills, covering continents of unending mountains and great oceans between them, with a stealthy yet dominating stride. In that dream the sky had fallen away before the lion's thrusting shoulders, the sky that somehow changed into the lion, and yet formed a background to its movement: and the sun had sometimes been rolling round and round it, as if it were a yellow ball, and sometimes had been fixed millions of miles away, but fixed as if it had been left like a lump of meat for the great beast; and Anthony had felt an anxious intense desire to run a few millions of miles in order to pull it down and save it from those jaws. Only however fast he ran he couldn't catch up with the lion's much slower movement. He ran much faster than the lion, but he couldn't get wherever it was so quickly, although of course the lion was farther away. But the farther away it was the bigger it was, according to the new rules of perspective, Anthony remembered himself seriously thinking. It had seemed extremely important to know the rules in that very muddled dream.

It had certainly been a lion—in the dream and in the garden. And he could not pretend—not even for Quentin— that the lioness had mattered nearly so much. So he said, "It was certainly a lioness in the road."

47

"And in the garden," Quentin exclaimed. "Why, surely yesterday morning you agreed it must have been a lioness in the garden."

"As a great and wise publisher whom I used to know once said," Anthony remarked, " 'I will believe anything of my past opinions.' But honestly—in the garden? I don't suppose it matters one way or the other, and very likely you're right."

"But what do you think? Don't you think it was a lioness?" Quentin cried. And "No," Anthony said obstinately, "I think it was a lion. I also think", he added with some haste, "I must have been wrong, because it couldn't have been. So there we are."

Quentin shrank back in his chair and Anthony cursed himself for being such a pig-headed precisian. But still, was it any conceivable good pretending—if the intellect had any authority at all? if there were any place for accuracy? In personal relationships it might, for dear love's sake, sometimes be necessary to lie, so complicated as they often were. But this, so far as Anthony could see, was a mere matter of a line to left or to right upon the wall, and his whole mind revolted at falsehood upon abstract things. It was like an insult to a geometrical pattern. Also he felt that it was up to Quentin—up to him just a little—to deal with this thing. If only he himself knew what his friend feared!

Quentin unintentionally answered his thought. "I've always been afraid," he said bitterly, "at school and at the office and everywhere. And I suppose this damned thing has got me in the same way somehow."

"The lion?" Anthony asked. Certainly it was a curious world.

"It isn't—it isn't just a lion," Quentin said. "Whoever saw a lion come from nowhere? But we did; I know we did, and you said so. It's something else—I don't know what"—he sprang again to his feet—"but it's something else. And it's after me."

"Look here, old thing," Anthony said, "let's talk it out. Good God, shall there be anything known to you or me that

48

we can't talk into comprehension between us? Have a cigarette, and let's be comfortable. It's only nine."

Quentin smiled rather wanly. "O let's try," he said. "Can you talk Damaris into comprehension?"

The remark was more direct than either of the two usually allowed himself, without an implicit invitation, but Anthony accepted it. "You've often talked me into a better comprehension of Damaris," he said.

"Theoretically," Quentin sneered at himself.

"Well, you can hardly tell that, can you?" Anthony argued. "If your intellect elucidated Da—— O damn!"

The bell of the front door had suddenly sounded and Quentin shied violently, dropping his cigarette. "God curse it," he cried out.

"All right," Anthony said, "I'll go. If it's anyone we know I won't let him in, and if it's anyone we don't know I'll keep him out. There! Look after that cigarette!" He disappeared from the room, and it was some time before he returned.

When he did so he was, in spite of his promise, accompanied. A rather short, thickset man, with a firm face and large eyes, was with him.

"I changed my mind, after all," Anthony said. "Quentin, this is Mr. Foster of Smetham, and he's come to talk about the lion too. So he was good enough to come up."

Quentin's habitual politeness, returning from wherever it hid during his intimacy with his friend, controlled him and said and did the usual things. When they were all sitting down, "And now let's have it," Anthony said. "Will you tell Mr. Sabot here what you have told me?"

"I was talking to Miss Tighe this afternoon," Mr. Foster said; he had a rough deep voice, Quentin thought, "and she told me that you gentlemen had been there two days ago—at Mr. Berringer's house, I mean—when all this began. So in view of what's happened since, I thought it would do no harm if we compared notes."

"When you say what's happened since," Anthony asked, "you mean the business at the meeting last night? I understood from Miss Tighe that one of the ladies there thought she saw a snake."

"I think—and she thinks—she *did* see a snake," Mr. Foster answered. "As much as Mr. Tighe saw the butterflies this afternoon. You won't deny them?"

"Butterflies?" Quentin asked, as Anthony shook his head, and then, with a light movement of it, invited Mr. Foster to explain.

"Mr. Tighe came in while I was at his house this afternoon," the visitor said, "in a very remarkable state of exaltation. He told us—Miss Tighe and myself—that he had been shown that butterflies were really true. Miss Tighe was inclined to be a little impatient, but I prevailed on her to let him tell us—or rather he insisted on telling us—what he had seen. As far as I could follow, there had been one great butterfly into which the lesser ones had passed. But Mr. Tighe took this to be a justification of his belief in them. He was very highly moved, he quite put us on one side, which is (if I may say so) unusual in so quiet a man as he, and he would do nothing but go to his cabinets and look at the collection of his butterflies. I left him", Mr. Foster ended abruptly, "on his knees, apparently praying to them."

Quentin had been entirely distracted by this tale from his own preoccupation. "*Praying!*" he exclaimed. "But I don't . . . Weren't you with him, Anthony?"

"I was up to a point," Anthony said. "I was going to tell you later on, whenever it seemed convenient. Mr. Foster is quite right. It can't possibly have been so, but we saw thousands and thousands of them all flying to one huge fellow in the middle, and then—well, then they weren't there."

"So Tighe said," Mr. Foster remarked. "But why can't it possibly have happened?"

"Because—because it can't," Anthony said. "Thousands of butterflies swallowed up in one, indeed!"

"There was Aaron's rod," Mr Foster put in, and for a moment perplexed both his hearers. Anthony, recovering first, said: "What, the one that was turned into a snake and swallowed the other snakes?"

"Exactly," Mr. Foster answered. "A snake."

"But you don't mean that this woman—what was her name? —that this Miss Wilmot saw Aaron's rod or snake, or what not, do you?" Anthony asked. And yet, Quentin thought, not with such amused scorn as might have been expected; it sounded more like the precise question which the words made it: "do you mean this?"

"I think the magicians of Pharaoh may have seen Miss Wilmot's snake," Mr. Foster said, "and all their shapely wisdom have been swallowed by it, as the butterflies of the fields were taken into that butterfly this afternoon."

"And to what was Mr. Tighe praying then?" Anthony said, his eyes intently fixed on the other.

"To the gods that he knew," Mr. Foster said, "or to such images of them as he had collected to give himself joy."

"The gods?" Anthony asked.

"That is why I have come here," Mr. Foster answered, "to find out what you know of them."

"Aren't we," Quentin put in, his voice sounding unnatural to him as he spoke, "aren't we making a rather absurd fuss over a mistake? We", his gesture included his friend, "were rather tired. And it was dark. Or almost dark. And we were— we were not frightened: I am not frightened: but we were startled. And the old man fell. And we did not see clearly." The sentences came out in continuous barks.

Mr. Foster turned so suddenly in his chair that Anthony jumped. "And will you see clearly?" he demanded, thrusting his body and head forward towards Quentin. "Will you?"

"No," Quentin cried back at him. "I will not. I will see nothing of it, if I can help it. I won't, I tell you! And you can't make me. The lion himself can't make me."

51

"The lion!" Mr. Foster said. "Young man, do you really think to escape, if it is on your track?"

"It isn't on my track, I tell you," Quentin howled, jumping up. "How can it be? There isn't any—there never was any. I don't believe in these things. There's London and us and the things we know."

Anthony interfered. "That at least is true," he said. "There is London and us and what we know. But it can't hurt to find out exactly what we know, can it? I mean, we have always rather agreed about that, haven't we? Look here, Quentin, sit down and let me tell Mr. Foster what we thought—at the time —and for the time—that we saw. And you put me right if I go wrong."

"Carry on." Quentin, trembling all over, forced himself to say, turning as he did so to make a pretence of rearranging his chair. Anthony therefore recounted the story of the Tuesday evening and of how on the lawn of that house they had seen, as it seemed, the gigantic form of the lion. He did it as lightly as possible, but at best, in the excited atmosphere of the room, the tale took on the sound of some dark myth made visible to mortal and contemporary eyes. He himself, before he had finished, found himself in the midst of speaking eyeing with mingled alarm, fascination, and hope, the room before him, almost as if at any minute the presence should be manifested there.

"And after that," Mr. Foster said, "did you not hear the thunder?"

"Why, yes," the young men said together.

Mr. Foster made a contemptuous motion with his hand. "Thunder," he uttered scornfully. "That was no thunder; that was the roaring of the lion."

Quentin seemed to be sitting still by a tremendous effort. Anthony eyed his visitor steadily.

"Tell us what you mean," he said.

Mr. Foster sat forward. "You have heard of the owner of the

house?" he said. "Well, Berringer is a very wise man—you must not judge him by all that group who get about him—and he has made it his business to try and see the world of principles from which this world comes. He——"

Anthony's raised hand stopped him. "The world of principles?"

"He believes—and I believe it too," Mr. Foster said, "that this world is created, and all men and women are created, by the entrance of certain great principles into aboriginal matter. We call them by cold names; wisdom and courage and beauty and strength and so on, but actually they are very great and mighty Powers. It may be they are the angels and archangels of which the Christian Church talks—and Miss Damaris Tighe—I do not know. And when That which is behind them intends to put a new soul into matter it disposes them as it will, and by a peculiar mingling of them a child is born; and this is their concern with us, but what is their concern and business among themselves we cannot know. And by this gentle introduction of them, every time in a new and just proportion, mankind is maintained. In the animals they are less mingled, for there each is shown to us in his own becoming shape; those Powers are the archetypes of the beasts, and very much more, but we need not talk of that. Now this world in which they exist is truly a real world, and to see it is a very difficult and dangerous thing, but our master held that it could be done, and that the man was very wise who would consecrate himself to this end as part—and the chief part—of his duty on earth. He did this, and I, as much as I can, have done it."

"But I haven't done it," Anthony said. "And therefore how can that world—if there is one—be seen by me and people like me?"

"As for that," the other answered, "there are many people who have disciplined and trained themselves more than they know, but that is not the point now. I know that this man was able sometimes to see into that world, and contemplate the

53

awful and terrible things within it, feeding his soul on such visions; and he could even help others towards seeing it, as he has done me on occasions. But as I told you just now, since these powers exhibit their nature much more singly in the beasts, so there is a peculiar sympathy between the beasts and them. Generally, matter is the separation between all these animals which we know and the powers beyond. But if one of those animals should be brought within the terrific influence of one particular idea—to call it that—very specially felt through a man's intense concentration on it——"

He paused, and Anthony said: "What then?"

"Why then", the other said, "the matter of the beast might be changed into the image of the idea, and this world, following that one, might all be drawn into that other world. I think this is happening."

"O!" said Anthony, and sat down. Quentin was crouched deeply in his chair, his limbs drawn in, his face hidden in his arms, resting on the arm of the chair. A minute or two went by; then Anthony said—

"It's quite insane, of course; but, if it were true, why a lioness into a lion?"

"Because the temporal and spatial thing may be masculine or feminine, but the immortal being must in itself appear as masculine to us, if masculinity is consonant with its nature," Mr. Foster answered. "As, of course, supposing that we could call the lion strength or authority or something like that, it would be. But it is absurd to use such words about these forces, at all."

"It would be something", Anthony couldn't help saying, "to know the pet name of any force one happened to meet." But he spoke almost as if to prick on his incredulity, and neither he nor the others smiled. A much longer time passed now before anyone spoke: then Anthony asked another question.

"And what about Mr. Berringer himself?"

"We can't yet tell", Foster said, "what has happened to

54

him. Myself, for what it's worth, I think he's the focus of the movement; in some way we don't understand. It's through him that this world is passing into that. He and his house are the centre."

"Is that why everything happens in his garden?" Anthony asked.

"It is why everything *begins* to happen in his garden," Foster answered. "But it won't stop there. If I'm right, if all this world is passing into that, then the effects will be seen farther and farther away. Our knowledge will more and more be a knowledge of that and not of this—more and more everything will be received into its original, animals, vegetables, all the world but those individual results of interior Powers which are men."

Anthony missed part of this. "I can't believe it," he said. "If you're at all right, it would mean destruction. But you can't, you can't be."

"What did you see in the garden?" Foster demanded. "You know whether you believe in the shape that was there."

Quentin looked up and spoke harshly. "And what of men?" he asked.

"Some men will welcome it," Foster said. "As Mr. Tighe has done—as I shall do. And they will be joined to that Power which each of them best serves. Some will disbelieve in it—as I think Damaris Tighe does; but they will find then what they do believe. Some will hate it, and run from it—as you do. I cannot guess what will happen to them, except that they will be hunted. For nothing will escape."

"Cannot the breach be closed?" Anthony asked.

Mr. Foster laughed a little. "Are we to govern the principles of creation?" he retorted.

Anthony looked at him thoughtfully, and then said still quietly, "Well, we don't know till we try, do we?"

Quentin looked anxiously at him. "Do you think there's a chance?" he exclaimed.

Anthony said slowly, "You know, Quentin, I'm almost certain that Damaris will dislike it very much indeed. It will interfere with Abelard dreadfully. And of course you may remember that I promised to do everything I could to help her get her degree."

"Even", Mr. Foster asked sarcastically, "to ruling the various worlds of creation?"

"Everything," Anthony answered. "I don't know why this Mr. Berringer—no, but perhaps it wasn't his fault, which makes it worse—I don't know why this lioness should come upsetting us. You don't care for the notion yourself, Quentin, do you?"

"I hate—I hate it," Quentin said, controlling himself not unsuccessfully. Anthony looked back at Mr. Foster. "You get the idea?" he asked.

Their visitor again laughed a little. "You might as well try and stop daffodils growing," he said. "It's the law."

"If it is," Anthony agreed, "that settles it. But, my dear Mr. Foster, I must insist on being allowed to find out. Actually, of course, I feel that all this thesis of yours is, if you'll excuse me, pure bunk. But I've watched some curious things happen, and now you tell me of others. I should hate anything to worry Miss Tighe—seriously; a little worry might be a perfectly good thing for her. And Mr. Sabot doesn't want the lion, and Mr. Sabot and I have done our best for years to assist one another against undue interference."

"Interference!" Foster said, with another laugh.

"Well, you can hardly call it less, can you?" Anthony asked. "I gather you're on the side of the lion?"

"I am on the side of the things I have wanted to see," the other answered, "and if these Powers destroy the world, I am willing to be destroyed. I have given myself to them."

"Well, I haven't," Anthony said, getting up. "Not yet, anyhow. And Mr. Sabot hasn't, nor Miss Tighe."

"You fool," Foster said, "can you stand against them?"

The Two Camps

"If they are part of me, as you tell me, perhaps I might; I don't know," Anthony answered. "But if they are, then perhaps the authority which is in me over me shall be in me over them. I'm repeating myself, I beg your pardon."

Mr. Foster got up, with a not quite good-humoured smile. "You're like most of the world," he said, "you don't know necessity when you see it. Well, I'd better go now. Goodnight, and thank you." He looked at Quentin and offered him no word.

"Necessity, as no doubt Abelard said," Anthony remarked, "is the mother of invention—*invenio*, you know. The question is what shall I *venio in*. We're none of us clear about that, I think."

He drifted with their visitor to the hall, and returned to find Quentin again restlessly roaming about the room. "Look here," he said, "you go to bed, old thing."

"But what are you going to do?" Quentin asked wretchedly.

"O Lord," said Anthony, "how do I know? I'm going to sit and meditate. No, I don't want to talk any more and it's no use going to Smetham till I've got my ideas clearer. Damaris can fend for herself to-night; at the rate things are going there doesn't seem to be any immediate danger. O Lord, what danger can there be? Do go away, and let me think or I shall be no good to anyone. Was ever such a lion-hunt? Goodnight, and God bless you. If you're waking in the morning, I shall probably have gone first, so don't bother about calling me. Goodnight, my dear, don't worry—the young lion and the dragon will we tread underfoot."

Chapter Five

SERVILE FEAR

In the morning however it was Anthony who woke Quentin by entering his room before he was up—it might also be said before he slept, for what sleep he had was rather a sinking into silent terror than into normal repose. Anthony sat down on the bed and took a cigarette from a box on the table.

"Look here," he said, "I've been thinking it all over. What about us both going down again for the week-end, and having a look round?"

Quentin, taken aback, stared at him, and then, "Do you think so?" he asked.

"I think we might as well," Anthony said. "I should like to see Mr. Tighe again, and find out what he feels, and I should very much like to hear whether anyone else is seeing things. Besides, of course," he added, "Damaris. But I'd like it a great deal better if you came too."

As Quentin said nothing he went on, "Don't you think you might? It wouldn't be any more tiresome for you there, do you think? And we might, one way or another, get something clear. Do think about it. We've talked about ideas often enough, and we should be able to do something much better if we were together."

Quentin, a little pale, went on thinking; then he looked at Anthony with a smile. "Well, we might try," he said, "but if the lion is about you *will* have to save me."

"God knows what I should do!" Anthony answered, "but you could tell me what you wanted. If I go alone I shall always have to ring you up, and that'll take time. Imagine me among

lions and snakes and butterflies and smells, asking everything
to wait while I telephoned. Well, that's all right. I think I shall
go down to-day—after I've made arrangements at the office.
I suppose you can't come till to-morrow? About mid-day or
so?"

"If London's still here," Quentin said, again faintly smiling.
"Let me know where you're staying."

"I'll ring you up here to-night—say about nine," Anthony
answered. "I shan't do anything but hang round to-day, and
to-morrow we'll see."

So the arrangement was carried out, and on the Saturday
afternoon the two young men wandered out on to the Berringer
road, as Anthony called it. Past the Tighe house, past the
sedate public-house at the next corner, and the little Baptist
chapel almost at the end of the town, out between the hedges
they went, more silent than usual, more intensely alert in
feet and eyes. The sun was hot, June was drawing to a rich
close.

"And nothing fresh has happened?" Quentin said, after
they had for some time exchanged trivialities about nature,
the world, philosophy, and art.

"No," Anthony murmured thoughtfully, "nothing has happened exactly, unless—I don't really know if it could be called
a happening—but Mr. Tighe has given up entomology."

"But I thought he was so keen!" Quentin exclaimed.

"So he was," Anthony answered. "That's what makes it
funny. I called on him yesterday—yes, Quentin, I really did
call on *him*—and very tactfully asked him. . . . O this and that
and how he felt. He was sitting in the garden looking at the
sky. So he said he felt very well, and I asked him if he had been
out after butterflies during the day. He said, 'O no, I shan't
do that again.' I suppose I stared or said something or other,
because he looked round at me and said, 'But I've nothing to
do with them now.' Then he said, quite sweetly, 'I can see
now they were only an occupation.' I said: didn't he think it

might be quite a good idea to have an occupation? and he said: yes, he supposed it might be if you needed it, but he didn't. So then he went on looking at the sky, and I came away."

"And Damaris?" Quentin asked.

"O Damaris seemed all right," Anthony answered evasively. It was true that, in one sense of the words, Damaris *had* seemed all right. She had been in a state of extreme irritation with her father, and indeed with everybody. People had been calling— Mrs. Rockbotham to see her, Mr. Foster to see her father; she could get no peace. Time was going by, and she was continually being interrupted, and she had in consequence lost touch with the precise relationship of the theory of Pythagoras about number with certain sayings attributed to Abelard's master William of Champagne. Nobody seemed to have the least idea of the importance of a correct evaluation of the concentric cultural circles of Hellenic and pre-medieval cosmology. And now if her father were going to hang about the house all day! There appeared to have been a most unpleasant scene that morning between them, when Damaris had been compelled to grasp the fact that Mr. Tighe proposed to abandon practical entomology entirely. She had (Anthony had gathered) asked him what he proposed to do—to which he had replied that there was no need to do anything. She had warned him that she herself must not be interrupted—to which again he had said merely: "No, no, my dear, go on playing, but take care you don't hurt yourself." At this Damaris had entirely lost her temper—not that she had said so in so many words, but Anthony quite justly interpreted her 'I had to speak pretty plainly to him,' as meaning that.

In consequence he had not been able to do more than hint very vaguely at Mr. Foster's theories. Theories which were interesting in Plato became silly when regarded as having anything to do with actual occurrences. Philosophy was a subject—her subject; and it would have been ridiculous to think of her subject as getting out of hand. Or her father, for that matter; only he was.

Anthony would have been delighted to feel that she was right; she was, of course, right. But he did uneasily feel that she was a little out of touch with philosophy. He had done his best to train his own mind to regard philosophy as something greater and more important than itself. Damaris, who adopted that as an axiom of speech, never seemed to follow it as a maxim of intellectual behaviour. If philosophies could get out of hand . . . he looked unhappily at the Berringer house as they drew near to it.

But at the gate both he and Quentin exclaimed. The garden was changed. The flowers were withered, the grass was dry and brown; in places the earth showed, hard and cracked. The place looked as if a hot sun had blazed on it for weeks without intermission. Everything living was dead within its borders, and (they noticed) for a little way beyond its borders. The hedges were leafless and brittle; the very air seemed hotter than even the June day could justify. Anthony drew a deep breath.

"My God, how hot it is!" he said.

Quentin touched the gate. "It *is* hot," he said. "I didn't notice it so much when we were walking."

"No," Anthony answered. "I don't, you know, think it was so hot there. This place is beginning"—he had been on the point of saying "to terrify me," when he remembered Quentin and changed it into "to seem quite funny." His friend however took no notice even of this; he was far too occupied in maintaining an apparently casual demeanour, of which his pallid cheeks, quick breathing, and nervous movements showed the strain. Anthony turned round and leant against the gate with his back to the house.

"It looks quiet and ordinary enough," he said.

The fields stretched up before them, meadow and cornfield in a gentle slope; along the top of the rising ground lay a series of groups of trees. The road on their left ran straight on for some quarter of a mile, then it swept round towards the right and itself climbed the hill, which it crossed beyond the last fragments of the scattered wood. The house by which they stood was indeed almost directly in the middle of a circular dip in the countryside. In one of the fields a number of sheep were feeding. Anthony's eyes rested on them.

"They don't seem to have been disturbed," he said.

"What do you really think about it all?" Quentin asked suddenly. "It's all nonsense, isn't it?"

Anthony answered thoughtfully. "I should think it was all nonsense if we hadn't both thought we saw the lion—and if I and Damaris's father hadn't both thought we saw the butterflies. But I really can't see how to get over that."

"But *is* the world slipping?" Quentin exclaimed. "Look at it. Is it?"

"No, of course not," Anthony said. "But—I don't want to be silly, you know—but, if we were to believe what the Foster fellow said, it wouldn't be that kind of slipping anyhow. It'd be more like something behind coming out into the open. And as I got him, all the more quickly when there are material forms to help it. The lioness was the first chance, and I suppose the butterflies were the next easiest—the next thing at hand."

"What about birds?" Quentin asked.

"I thought of them," Anthony said, "and—look here, we'd better talk it out, so I'll tell you—— It's a minor matter, and I daresay I shouldn't have noticed them, but as a matter of fact, I haven't seen or heard any birds round here at all."

Quentin took this calmly. "Well, we don't notice them much, do we?" he said. "And what about the sheep?"

"The sheep I give you," Anthony answered. "Either Foster's mad, or else there must be something to explain that. Perhaps there isn't an Archetypal Sheep." His voice was steady, and he smiled, but the mild jest fell very flat.

Servile Fear

"And what", Quentin asked, "do you think of doing?"

Anthony turned to face him. "I think you've probably seen it too," he said. "I'm going to do my best to find that lion."

"Why?" the other asked.

"Because—if it were true—we must meet it," Anthony said, "and I will have a word in the meeting."

"You do believe it," Quentin said.

"I can't entirely disbelieve it without refusing to believe in ideas," Anthony answered, "and I can't do that. I can't go back on the notion that all these abstractions do mean something important to us. And mayn't they have a way of existing that I didn't know? Haven't we agreed about the importance of ideas often enough?"

"But ideas——" Quentin began, and stopped. "You're right, of course," he added. "If this is so we must be prepared— if we meant anything."

"And as we certainly meant something——" Anthony said, relaxing to his former position. "My God, look!"

Up on the top of the rise the lion was moving. It was passing slowly along among the trees, now a little this side, now hidden by the trunks—or partly hidden. For its gigantic and golden body, its enormous head and terrific mane, were of too vast proportions to be hidden. It moved with a kind of stately ferocity, its eyes fixed in front of it, though every now and then its head turned one way or the other, in an awful ease. Once its eyes seemed to pass over the two young men, but if it saw them it ignored them, and proceeded slowly upon its own path. Half terrified, half attracted, they gazed at it.

Quentin moved suddenly, "O let's get away!"

Anthony's hand closed on his arm. "No," he said, though his voice shook, "we're going up that road to meet it. Or else I shall never be able to speak of ideas and truths again. Come along."

"I daren't," Quentin muttered shrinking.

"But what's lucidity then?" Anthony asked. "Let's be as quick as we can. For if that is what is in me, then I may be able to control it; and if not——"

"Yes, if not——" Quentin cried out.

"Then we will see what a Service revolver will do," Anthony answered, putting his hand in the pocket of his loose coat. "One way or the other. Come on."

Quentin moved unhappily, but he did not refuse. Their eyes still set on the monster, they left the gate and went on along the road; and up on the ridge it continued its own steady progress. The trees however after a few minutes shut it out of their sight, and even when they came round the curve in the road and began to move up the gentle rise they did not again see it. This added to the strain of expectation they both felt, and as they stepped on Quentin exclaimed suddenly: "Even·if it's what you say, how do you know you were *meant* to see it? We're only men—how should we be meant to look at—these things?"

"The face of God . . ." Anthony murmured. "Well, even now perhaps I'd as soon die that way as any. But Tighe didn't die when he saw the butterfly, nor we when we saw it before."

"But it's madness to go like this and *look* for it," Quentin said. "I daren't, that's the truth, if you want it. I daren't. I can't." He stood still, trembling violently.

"I don't know that I *dare* exactly," Anthony said, also pausing. "But I shall. What the devil's that?"

It was not the form of the lion but the road some little distance in front of them at which he was staring. For across it, almost where it topped the rise and disappeared down the other side, there passed a continuous steady ripple. It seemed to be moving crosswise; wave after gentle wave followed each other from the fields on one side to the fields opposite; they could see the disturbed dust shaken off and up, and settling again only to be again disturbed. The movement did not stop at the road-side, it seemed to pass on into the fields, and be there lost to sight. The two young men stood staring.

"The damn road's moving!" Anthony exclaimed, as if driven to unwilling assent.

Quentin began to laugh, as he had laughed that other evening, hysterically, madly. "Quite right," he shrieked in the midst of his laughter, "quite right, Anthony. The road's moving: didn't you know it would? It's scratching its own back or something. Let's help it, shall we?"

"Don't be a bloody fool," Anthony cried to him. "Stop it, Quentin, before I knock you silly."

"Ha!" said Quentin with another shriek, "I'll show you what's silly. It isn't us! it's the world! The earth's mad, didn't you know? All mad underneath. It pretends to behave properly, like you and me, but really it's as mad as we are! And now it's beginning to break out. Look, Anthony, we're the first to see the earth going quite, quite mad. That's your bright idea, that's what you're running uphill to see. Wait till you feel it in you!"

He had run a few steps on as he talked, and now paused with his head tossed up, his feet pirouetting, his mouth emitting fresh outbursts of laughter. Anthony felt his own steadiness beginning to give way. He looked up at the sky and the strong afternoon sun—in that at least there was as yet no change. High above him some winged thing went through the air; he could not tell what it was but he felt comforted to see it. He was not entirely alone, it seemed; the pure balance of that distant flight entered into him as if it had been salvation. It was incredible that life should sustain itself by such equipoise, so lightly, so dangerously, but it did, and darted onward to its purpose so. His mind and body rose to the challenging revelation; the bird, whatever it was, disappeared in the blue sky in a moment, and Anthony, curiously calmed, looked back at the earth in front of him. Across the road the movement was still passing, but it seemed smaller, and even while he looked it had ceased. Still and motionless the road stretched in front of him, and though his blood was running cold his eyes were quiet as he turned them on his friend.

Quentin jerked his head. "You think it's stopped, don't you?" he jeered. "You great fool, wait, only wait! I haven't told you, but I've known it a long time. I've heard it when I lay awake at night, the earth chuckling away at its imbecile jokes. It's slobbering over us now. O you're going to find out things soon! Wait till it scratches you. Haven't you felt it scratching you when you thought about that woman, you fool? When you can't sleep for thinking of her? and the earth scratches you again? Ho, and you didn't know what it was. But I know."

Anthony looked at him long and equably. "You know, Quentin," he said, "you *do* have the most marvellous notions. When I think that I really know you I get almost proud. The beauty of it is that for all I know you're right, only if you are there's nothing for us to discuss. And though I don't say there is, I insist on behaving as if there was. Because I will not believe in a world where you and I can't talk." He came a step nearer and added: "Will you? It'll be an awful nuisance for me if you do."

Quentin had stopped pirouetting and was swinging to and fro on his toes. "Talk!" he said uncertainly. "What's the good of talking when the earth's mad?"

"It supports the wings in the air," Anthony answered. "Come along and support."

He tucked his arm into his friend's. "But perhaps for this afternoon——" he began, and paused, arrested by the other's face. Quentin had looked back over his shoulder, and his eyes were growing blind with terror. Sense and intelligence deserted them; Anthony saw and swung round. By the side of the road, almost where the ripple had seemed to pass over, there appeared the creature they had set out to seek. It was larger and mightier than when they had seen it before—and, comparatively close as they now were, they fell back appalled by the mere effluence of strength that issued from it. It was moving like a walled city, like the siege-towers raised against Nineveh or Jerusalem; each terrible paw, as it set it down, sank into the firm ground as if into mud, but was plucked forth without effort; the movement of its mane, whenever it mightily turned its head, sent reverberations of energy through the air, which was shaken into wind by that tossed hair. Anthony's hand rested helplessly on his revolver, but he could not use it—whether this were mortal lion or no, he must take his chance, its being to his exposed being. He had challenged the encounter, and now it was upon him, and all the strength of his body was flowing out of him: he was beginning to tremble and gasp. He no longer had hold of Quentin, nor was indeed aware of him; a faintness was taking him—perhaps this was death, he thought, and then was suddenly recalled to something like consciousness by hearing a shot at his side.

Quentin had snatched the revolver from him and was firing madly at the lion, screaming, "There! there! there!" as he did so, screaming in a weakness that seemed to lay him appallingly open to the advance of that great god—for it looked no less—whenever it should choose to crush him. The noise sounded as futile as the bullets obviously proved, and the futility of the outrage awoke in Anthony a quick protest.

"Don't!" he cried out, "you're giving in. That's not the way to rule; that's not within you." To keep himself steady, to know somehow within himself what was happening, to find the capacity of his manhood even here—some desire of such an obscure nature stirred in him as he spoke. He felt as if he were riding against some terrific wind; he was balancing upon the instinctive powers of his spirit; he did not fight this awful opposition but poised himself within and above it. He heard vaguely the sound of running feet and knew that Quentin had fled, but he himself could not move. It was impossible now to help others; the overbearing pressure was seizing and stifling his breath; and still as the striving force caught him he refused to fall and strove again to overpass it by rising into the balance of adjusted movement. "If this is in me I reach beyond it," he cried to himself again, and felt a new-come freedom answer his cry. A memory—of all insane things—awoke in him of the flying he had done in the last year of the war; it seemed as if again he looked down on a wide stretch of land and sea, but no human habitations were there, only forest, and plain, and river, and huge saurians creeping slowly up from the waters, and here and there other giant beasts coming into sight for a moment and then disappearing. Another flying thing went past below him—a hideous shape that was a mockery of the clear air in which he was riding, riding in a machine that, without his control, was now sweeping down towards the ground. He was plunging towards a prehistoric world; a lumbering vastidity went over an open space far in front, and behind it his own world broke again into being through that other. There was a wild minute in which the two were mingled; mammoths and dinotheria wandered among hedges of English fields, and in that confused vision he felt the machine make easy landing, run, and come to a stop. Yet it couldn't have been a machine, for he was no longer in it; he hadn't got out, but he was somehow lying on the ground, drawing deep breaths of mingled terror and gratitude and salvation at last. In a recovered peace he moved, and found that he was actually stretched at the side of the road; he moved again and sat up.

There was no sign of the lion, nor of Quentin. He got to his feet; all the countryside lay still and empty, only high above him a winged something still disported itself in the full blaze of the sun.

Chapter Six

MEDITATION OF
MR. ANTHONY DURRANT

When at last, by another road, Anthony returned to Smetham he was very tired. It was not the extra length of the journey that had tired him—he had not at that moment been able to bring himself to go back by Berringer's home—but a shock of wrestling with a great strength. He had taken long to recover his usual equilibrium, and he had been worried over Quentin. But no gazing from the top of the ridge had revealed his friend to him, and there was no sign to show in which direction the fugitive had gone. It was a small comfort to Anthony to remember that he had actually heard the flying feet, for the horrible possibility haunted him that Quentin might . . . might have been destroyed—shattered or annihilated by the powers which, it seemed, were finding place in the world, or perhaps it would be truer to say (if Foster had been right) into whose dominion the outer world was passing. But the thought of Foster reminded him of another phrase; the man had said something about those who hated and feared it being hunted. Was it possible that such a chase was even now proceeding? that over those sedate hills, and among those quiet cornfields and meadows, a golden majesty was with inexorable speed pursuing Quentin's fearful and lunatic haste? a haste which could find no shelter, nor set any barrier between itself and its fate? The distress of such a thought swelled in Anthony's heart, as, heavily and slowly, he came back to the town. For he, it was evident, could at that time do nothing; he was far too exhausted, and he needed to be alone in order to realize what had happened, and what his next action should be. Besides, always and everywhere, thrusting between even Quentin's need and any possibility of succour, there was Damaris.

He bathed and rested, and ate and drank, and then feeling better went out to smoke and think in the grounds of the hotel.

It was still early evening; tennis was going on not far off, but presently everyone would be going in to dinner. Anthony found a deck chair in a remote corner, sat down, lit a cigarette, and began to meditate. He arranged his questions in his mind —six of them:

1. Had it happened?
2. Why had it happened?
3. What was likely to happen now?
4. How was it likely to affect Damaris?
5. What was happening to Quentin?
6. What did he himself propose to do about it all?

Over the first question he spent no time. The things that he had seen had been as real to him as anything that he had ever seen. Besides, Tighe had given up collecting butterflies, and Foster had come and talked with him, and Quentin had run away—all because of various aspects of "it." If "it" hadn't happened, then Quentin had been right and they were all going mad together. The fact that most of Smetham knew nothing about it and wouldn't have believed it was irrelevant. He could act only upon his own experience, and his actions should be, as far as possible, consistent with that experience. "It" then had happened. But why? or, to put it another way, what was happening? Here he had no hypothesis of his own, and only one of anyone else's—Foster's: that between a world of living principles, existing in its own state of being, and this present world, a breach had been made. The lioness from without, the lion from—within? say within, it meant as much as any other mode of description—had approached each other through the channel of a man's consciousness, and had come together by the natural kinship between the material image and the immaterial idea. And after that first impact others had followed; other principles had found their symbols and possessed them, drawing back into themselves as many of those particular symbols as came immediately within the zone influenced. How far those presences could be seen by men he could not guess; he and Quentin had seen the lion, he and Tighe the butterfly. But Foster had told him how one woman, and only one, had cried out that she had seen a snake, which Foster himself had not seen. What then was the distinction? Pondering over this, it occurred to him suddenly that snakes were not as common as butterflies in England, and that only a most unusual chance had loosed a lioness on that country road. Might it not be then that these powers were not visible till they had found their images? not visible at least to ordinary eyes? Why that woman had seen one he did not profess to explain. Nor why, lioness and butterflies being gone, the many sheep he had seen still remained quietly feeding near the house of exodus. He remembered with a shock the strange quiver that had passed across the road that afternoon; was it so certain that he had *not* seen some movement of the snake? If the long undulating body had passed through the earth—if the earth, so to speak, had been charged with that serpentine influence? . . . All this was beyond him; he could not tell. But, right or wrong, there seemed to him at present no other hypothesis than that of powers loosed into the world; without finally believing it, he accepted it until he should discover more.

And what was likely to happen now? Anthony threw away the end of his cigarette, and sighed. Why did he always ask himself these silly questions? Always intellectualizing, he thought, always trying to find a pattern. Well, and why not? If Foster was right, every man—he himself—was precisely a pattern of these powers. But it wasn't at the moment his own, it was the general pattern he was concerned with. The word supplied a possible answer—the present general pattern of the

world was being violently changed into another pattern, perhaps a better one, perhaps not, but anyhow another. And the
present pattern looked like being utterly and entirely destroyed, if the world went on passing into that other state.
Something had saved him that afternoon, but as he recalled his
breathless struggle with overwhelming energy he realized part
of the danger that was drawing near. The beauty of butterflies
was one thing, but what if these principles drew to their separate selves the elements of which each man was made? Man, it
seemed to Anthony, looked like having a thin time. If the
animals were swallowed up as Aaron's snake swallowed the
snakes of the magicians? Were the other plagues, he wondered,
but the permitted domination of some element by its own or
another principle? Was that principle—whatever it might be
—that knew itself in the frog loosed once in all the palaces of
Egypt? and did the life which is in blood enter into and control
the waters of the Nile? As perhaps on a later day at Cana
ecstasy which is wine entered into lucidity which is water and
possessed it? "Damn!" said Anthony, "I'm romancing, and
anyhow it doesn't matter; it's got nothing to do with what is
happening now. It was the lion that began it here and (if
they're right) the snake. Is the lion still beginning it?"

He sat up in some excitement. They had seemed to see the
shape of the lion moving slowly—and the queer wave in the
road had passed almost in the same path but in the opposite
direction. Was this the place of entrance?—were those two the
guards of the other world, the dwellers on that supernatural
threshold, pacing round in widening circles, until slowly the
whole world was encompassed? And, in that case, how long
before their circle included Smetham—and Damaris?

He was up against his fourth question, and he made himself
lean back to look at it quietly. But his heart was beating
quickly, and his hands moved restlessly about his chair. How
would it affect Damaris? He tried to see her again as she was
in her own nature—he tried to think to which of these august

powers she was kin; but he could do not it. "O Damaris darling!" he exclaimed, and felt himself in all a terrible fear for her. If that childish ignorance and concern and childish arrogance and selfishness met these dangers—O then what shelter, what safety, would there be? He wanted to help her, he wanted to stay this new movement till she had understood, and turned to meet it; and if his mind clamoured again with a desire that they should do this together, and together find the right way into or out of this other world—if so far his own self thrust into his otherwise selfless anxiety, it was a momentary accompaniment. But she wouldn't, she would go on thoughtfully playing with the dead pictures of ideas, with names and philosophies, Plato and Pythagoras and Anselm and Abelard, Athens and Alexandria and Paris, not knowing that the living existences to which seers and saints had looked were already in movement to avenge themselves on her. "O you sweet blasphemer!" Anthony moaned, "can't you wake?" Gnostic traditions, medieval rituals, Aeons and Archangels—they were cards she was playing in her own game. But she didn't know, she didn't understand. It wasn't her fault; it was the fault of her time, her culture, her education—the pseudo-knowledge that affected all the learned, the pseudo-scepticism that infected all the unlearned, in an age of pretence, and she was only pretending as everybody else did in this lost and imbecile century. Well, it was up to him to do something.

But what? He could, he would, go and see her. But what could he do to ensure her safety? Could he get her to London? It would be difficult to persuade her, and if he put it to the touch by attempting to compel her and failed—that would be worse than all. Damaris was still keeping herself at a distance; her feeling for him was stilled and directed by her feeling for herself. He had the irresistible force all right, but honesty compelled him to admit that she, as an immovable object, was out of its direct line. Besides—London? If this kind of thing was going on, supposing (just for one split second) that Foster's fantastic hypotheses was right, what would be the good of London? Sooner or later London too would slip in and be subject to great animals—the fierceness of the wolf would threaten it from Hampstead, the patience of the tortoise would wait beyond Streatham and Richmond; and between them the elk and the bear would stalk and lumber, drawing the qualities out of mankind, terrifying, hunting down, destroying. He did not know how swiftly the process of absorption was going on— a week might see that golden mane shaken over London from Kensal Rise. London was no good, his thought raced on, no, nor any other place then; no seas or mountains could avail. Still, if he could persuade her to move for a few days—that would give him time to do something. And at that he came up against the renewed memory of Foster's scornful question. Was he really proposing to govern the principles of creation? to attempt to turn back, for the sake of one half-educated woman's personal safety, the movement of the vast originals of all life? How was he, he thought despairingly, to close the breach, he who had that very afternoon been swept almost into death by the effluence from but one visioned greatness? It was hopeless, it was insane, and yet the attempt had to be made.

Besides, there.was Quentin. He had small expectation of being of any use to Quentin, but somewhere in this neighbour-hood his unhappy friend—if he lived yet—was wandering, and Anthony disliked going off himself while the other's doom re-mained unknown. And there might be some way—this Ber-ringer now; perhaps something more could be found out about him. If he had opened, might he not close? Or his friends— this infernal group? Some of them might help: they couldn't all want Archetypes coming down on them, not if they were like most of the religious people he had met. They also prob-ably liked their religion taken mild—a pious hope, a devout ejaculation, a general sympathetic sense of a kindly universe— but nothing upsetting or bewildering, no agony, no darkness, no uncreated light. Perhaps he had better go and see some of them—Foster again, or even this Miss Wilmot, or the doctor who was attending Berringer, and whose wife had got Damaris (so she had told him) into this infernal mess. Yes, and then to persuade Damaris to go to London; and to look for Quentin...

And all the while to be quiet and steady, to remember that man was meant to control, to be lord of his own nature, to accept the authority that had been given to Adam over all manner of beasts, as the antique fables reported, and to exercise that authority over the giants and gods which were threatening the world.

Anthony sighed a little and stood up. "Adam," he said, "Adam. Well, I am as much a child of Adam as any. The Red Earth is a little pale perhaps. Let's go and walk in the garden among the beasts of the field which the Lord God hath made. I feel a trifle microcosmic, but if the proportion is in me let these others know it. Let me take the dominion over them—I wish I had any prospect of exercising dominion over Damaris."

Chapter Seven

INVESTIGATIONS INTO A RELIGION

D r. Rockbotham leaned back and looked at his watch. Mrs. Rockbotham looked at him. Dinner was just over; in a quarter of an hour he had to be in his surgery. The maid entered the room with a card on a salver. Dr. Rockbotham took it.

"Anthony Durrant," he read out and looked over at his wife enquiringly. She thought and shook her head.

"No," she began, and then "O wait a minute! Yes, I believe I do remember. He's one of my cousin's people on *The Two Camps*. I met him there once."

"He's very anxious to see you, sir," the maid said.

"But what can he want?" Dr. Rockbotham asked his wife. "If you know him, Elise, you'd better come along and see him too. I can't give him very long now, and I've had a tiring day. Really, people do come at the most inconvenient times."

His protest however was only half-serious, and he turned a benign face on Anthony in the drawing-room. "Mr. Durrant? My wife thinks she remembers you, Mr. Durrant. You're on *The Two Camps*, aren't you? Yes, yes. Well, as you've met there's no need for introductions. Sit down, do. And what can we do for you, Mr. Durrant?"

"I've really only called to ask—if I may—a question about Mr. Berringer," Anthony said. "We heard in London that he was very ill, and as he's a person of some importance" (this, he thought guiltily, is the Archetypal Lie) "I thought I'd run down and enquire. As a matter of fact, there was some sort of idea that he should do a series of articles for us on . . . on the symbolism of the cosmic myths."

Mrs. Rockbotham nodded in pleasure. "I mentioned something of the sort to my cousin once," she said. "I'm delighted to find that he followed it up. An excellent idea."

Anthony's heart sank a little; he foresaw, if the world were not swallowed up, some difficulty in the future. "We were", he said, "so sorry to hear he was ill. The housekeeper didn't seem to know much, and as Mr. Tighe—whom you know, I think— mentioned that you were attending him, I ventured . . ."

"Certainly, certainly," Dr. Rockbotham said. "These notorieties, eh? Famous men, and so on. Well, yes. I'm afraid he is ill."

"Seriously?" Anthony asked.

"O well, seriously——" The doctor paused. "An affection of the brain, I very much fear. He's more or less in a state of unconsciousness, and of course in such cases it's a little difficult to explain in non-technical language. A nurse has been installed, and I'm keeping a careful watch. If necessary I shall take the responsibility of getting another opinion. You don't, I suppose, know the name or address of any of his friends or his solicitor, do you?"

"I'm afraid not," Anthony said.

"It's a little difficult position," Dr. Rockbotham went on. "His housekeeper knows of no one; of course I haven't looked at his papers yet . . . if I could get in touch with anyone . . ."

"If I can do anything——" Anthony offered. "But I've no personal acquaintance with Mr. Berringer; only a general knowledge of his name." And that, he thought, only since the day before yesterday. But he wasn't going to stick at trifles now.

"My dear," said Mrs. Rockbotham, "perhaps Mr. Durrant would like to see Mr. Berringer."

"I don't see that Mr. Durrant would gain much by that," the doctor answered. "He's lying perfectly still and unconscious. But if", he went on to the young man, "I may take it that you represent a widespread concern . . ."

"I represent", Anthony said, "what I believe may be a very widespread concern." It seemed to him utterly ridiculous to be talking like this, but he couldn't burst out on these two people with his supernatural menagerie. And yet this woman ought to have realized something.

". . . don't know that I wouldn't welcome your association," Dr. Rockbotham concluded. "We professional men have to be so careful. If you'd care to come out with me to-morrow morning—about twelve——?"

"I should be"—no, Anthony felt he couldn't say delighted or pleased at going back to that house—"honoured." Honoured! "What's honour? . . . Who hath it? he that died o' Wednesday." "I shouldn't be a bit surprised if I ended by being he that died o' Wednesday," he thought grimly.

"Why, that will be capital," the doctor said, "and we can see what's best to do. You'll excuse me, won't you? I have to get to the surgery."

"Don't go, Mr. Durrant," Mrs. Rockbotham said, as Anthony rose. "Sit down and tell me how things are with *The Two Camps*."

Anthony obediently sat down, and told his hostess as much as he thought good for her about the present state of the periodical. He persevered at the same time in bringing the conversation as close as possible to the collapse of Mr. Berringer and the last monthly meeting of the Group. Mrs. Rockbotham was very willing to talk about it.

"Most disconcerting for Miss Tighe," she said, "though I must say she behaved very charmingly about it. So good-natured. Of course no one had any idea that Dora Wilmot would go off like that."

"Miss Wilmot is a friend of yours?" Anthony threw in casually.

"We've been connected in a number of things," Mrs. Rockbotham admitted, "the social fêtes every summer and this Study Group and the Conservative Committee. I remember she was a great deal of use with the correspondence at the time of the first Winter Lectures we got up to amuse the poorer people. I believe she went to some of them—a good simple soul. But this——!"

"She's belonged to the town for a good while?" Anthony asked.

"Born here," Mrs. Rockbotham said. "Lives in the white house at the upper corner of the market-place—you must have seen it. Just beyond Martin the bookseller's—his assistant was one of our Group too. I suppose Mr. Berringer invited him, though of course he was hardly of the same social class as most of us."

"Perhaps Mr. Berringer thought that the study of the world of principles——" Anthony allowed a gesture to complete his sentence.

"No doubt," Mrs. Rockbotham answered. "Though personally I always think it better and simpler if like sticks to like. It simply distracts one's attention if the man next you rattles his false teeth or can't get up from his chair easily."

"That", Anthony said, feeling that the confession was due to truth, "is undeniably so. Perhaps it means that we haven't got very far."

Mrs. Rockbotham shook her head. "It's always been so," she said, "and I shouldn't myself find I could concentrate nearly so well if Mr. Berringer hadn't shaved for a week. I don't see the smallest use in pretending that it isn't so."

"Didn't this young man—what did you say his name was?—shave then?" Anthony asked.

"Richardson—yes, of course—I was only illustrating," the lady said. "Well, if you must go——" as Anthony stood up firmly. "If you see Miss Tighe do tell her that I'm still ashamed."

"I'm sure Miss Tighe wouldn't wish you to be anything of the sort," Anthony lied with brazen politeness; and, treasuring his two pieces of information, departed. It was at least a small piece of luck that the two places were near together.

From outside the bookseller's he peered cautiously in. A nice-looking old gentleman was showing children's books to two ladies; a tall gaunt young man was putting other books into shelves. Anthony hoped that the first gentleman was Mr. Martin and the other Mr. Richardson. He went in with a quick determined step, and straight up to the young man, who turned to meet him.

"Have you by any chance an edition of St. Ignatius's treatise against the Gnostics?" he asked in a low clear voice.

The young assistant looked gravely back. "Not for sale, I'm afraid," he said. "Nor, if it comes to that, the Gnostic treatises against St. Ignatius."

"Quite," Anthony answered. "Are you Mr. Richardson?"

"Yes," the other said.

"Then I apologize and all that, but I should very much like to talk to you about modern Gnosticism or what appear to be its equivalents," Anthony said rapidly. "If you don't mind. I assure you I'm perfectly serious—though I do come from Mrs. Rockbotham. Would you, could you, spare me a little time?"

"Not here very well," Richardson said. "But if you could come round to my rooms about half-past nine, I should be glad to discuss anything with you—anything possible."

"So many things seem to be possible," Anthony murmured. "At half-past nine, then? And thank you. I'm not really being silly." He liked the other's equable reception of the intrusion, and the reserved watchfulness of his manner.

"17 Bypath Villas," Richardson said. "It's not more than ten minutes away. Along that street, down the second on the right, and then it's the third to the left. No, I'm afraid we haven't it"—this as Mr. Martin, having disposed of his own customers, was drawing near.

"Then", said Anthony, looking hastily round, with a vague sense of owing a return to the bookseller for the use he had made of the shop, "I'll have that." He picked up from a chance shelf of reduced library copies a volume with the title: *Mistresse of Majesty; the lives of seven beautiful women from Agnes Sorel to Mrs. Fitzherbert.* "But it's not very up-to-date, is it?" he added rather gloomily, as he took his change.

"The morality of the House of Windsor——" Richardson said, and bowed him out.

Tucking the book under his arm in some irritation, Anthony set out for Miss Wilmot's, and found it within a few steps. He rang the bell, and looked despairingly round to see if there were any way of disposing of *Mistresses of Majesty*, but the street-lamps were too bright and the passers-by too many. He was therefore still clutching it when he gave his name to the maid, and asked if Miss Wilmot could see him—"About Mr. Berringer," he added, thinking that would be as likely as anything to gain her attention.

The maid came back with instructions to show him in at once. He entered a small, neatly furnished room, and found not only a lady whom he assumed to be Miss Wilmot sitting by the window, but also a gentleman whom he knew to be Mr. Foster standing by her. He bowed gravely to them both.

"Do sit down, Mr. Durrant," the lady said.

Anthony obeyed, and looked rather thoughtfully at Mr. Foster, whose unexpected presence he felt might hamper his style. It was no use coming as an ignorant inquirer, nor even as a perplexed seeker; he hastily re-arranged his opening.

"So very kind of you to see me, Miss Wilmot," he began. "I expect Mr. Foster has told you what I really came to ask. I'm very anxious to find out two things as far as I can—first, what has happened to Mr. Berringer, and secondly, what happened on Wednesday night."

He studied Miss Wilmot as he spoke, with a feeling that she was somehow different from what he had expected. But so, he thought at the same minute, was Foster. There was something about the man that was more determined—almost more brutal—than had been before; the gaze that met his was almost fierce in its . . . its arrogance—that was the only word. The woman puzzled him; she was, in the queerest manner, gathered up in her chair—her eyes were half closed—her head every now and then swayed slightly. Nothing seemed to him less like what he had supposed the "good simple" creature of Mrs. Rockbotham's eulogy would be. But she said: "And what can *we* tell *you*, Mr. Durrant?" and he wondered if the question was, or was not, inflected with mockery.

"And why should we tell you, Mr. Durrant?" Foster said, sinking his head a little and raising his shoulders, as if the question sprang out of him with a sudden leap.

Anthony, sitting on a chair almost equidistant from both, said, "It seems more and more to be a matter of general importance."

"Ha!" Foster said, "you think that now, do you?"

"I think I never denied it," Anthony answered. "But I'm willing to admit that I'm much more inclined to accept your hypothesis than I was."

"Hypothesis!" Foster deeply exclaimed, and at the same time Miss Wilmot laughed, a little laugh of quiet amusement, which made Anthony move uneasily. Whatever the joke was he hadn't begun to see it. He suspected that he was the joke; well perhaps he was. Only he said, almost sharply: "But I believe in my own."

"And that is?" Miss Wilmot said softly.

"I believe", Anthony answered, looking straight at her, "that I must try myself against these things."

"And if they are in you how will you do it?" she asked, moving her head a little. "Will you set yourself against yourself? For without us you could not be, and if you struggle against us what shall triumph? Are you quite sure that you have anything which we can't take away? I think though you haven't gone far in your studies, Mr. Anthony Durrant, you would be very wise to ceas-s-se."

The last word indescribably prolonged itself in the twilight;

the sound ran round the walls as if the very room were alive with sibilants. But the noise was lost in the deep voice with which Foster, momently seen more darkly as a hunched shape against the open window, said: "Very wise."

Anthony jumped to his feet. "And what do you mean by that?" he said, staying himself from adding more by an interior warning against rhetoric or futility. So that, as if they waited for more, they did not for a moment answer him, and the three were suspended in expectation. As the pause lengthened Anthony felt a nervous anxiety grow in him, a longing to say something before anything could be said against him, to break into a braggadocio which would betray the weakness it pretended to hide. He bit his lip; his hands behind him drove the edge of *Mistresses of Majesty* into his back; he moved his feet farther apart to take a firmer stand. And then he met Dora Wilmot's eyes.

They were gazing at him as if they were following the helpless scurry of some escaping creature—a rabbit perhaps, and he felt the cunning of his restraint laid open to them. She knew all about him, all his ideas, his intentions, his efforts. His defiance was no subtlety but a mere silliness; his intellect acknowledged a greater power of intellect—or rather a something which passed through intellect. He felt like a student who paused before an expert, and in sheer hopelessness began to relax. The slight movement forward which Foster made escaped him; so did the other's slow raising of his hands till they came up almost level with the shoulders, and the elbows went back and the body crouched a little deeper—all this passed unseen. Anthony knew himself for a fool; he could do nothing; a cold shudder caught his ankles, his knees, and seized his whole body, till in that sudden trembling his hands opened and the book he carried fell with a thud to the floor. The shock of noise went through them all—Dora Wilmot leaned swiftly aside, Foster jerked himself back, and Anthony, violently released, brought his feet together and threw out his arms.

In that movement they were upon him. Quicker than he to recover, swifter than he to realize his escape, drawing more easily on the Powers they knew, they came at him while he still drew the first deep breath of release. The woman slid in one involved movement from the chair in which she had sat half-coiled, and from where she lay on the floor at his feet her arms went up, her hands clutching at his legs, and twisted themselves round his waist. At the same time the man sprang forward and upward, hands seizing Anthony's shoulders, head thrust forward as if in design upon his throat. Anthony was aware of their attack just before it caught him, hardly in time, yet just in time, to throw himself forward to meet it. His rising forearm struck the man's jaw with sufficient force to divert the head whose mouth champed viciously at him, but the woman's fast hold on his body prevented him from shaking himself free of the fingers that drove into his shoulders like claws. He heaved mightily forward, and drove upward again with his forearm, but their bodies were too close for him to get any force into the blow. His foot struck, stumbled, and as he freed and lifted it, trod on a rounded shape that writhed beneath it. All round him in the room were noises of hissing and snarling, and as he staggered aside in the effort to regain his footing the hot breath of one adversary panted into his face, so that it seemed to him as if he struggled in the bottom of some loathly pit where foul creatures fought for their prey. And he was their prey, unless . . . He felt himself falling, and cried out; the tightening pressure round his body choked the cry in mid-utterance, and something slid yet higher round his chest. In a tumultuous conflict he crashed to the ground, but sideways, so that as he lay he was able to twist himself face downwards and save his throat. He felt his collar wrenched off and nails tearing at his neck; a twisting weight writhed over him from his shoulders downwards. For a second he lay defeated, then all his spirit within him cried out "No," and thrust itself in that single syllable from his mouth. His arms at least had been freed in

his fall; he pressed his hands against the floor and with a terrific
effort half raised himself. The man creature, at this abandoning its tearing at his neck, came at him again from one side.
Anthony put all the energy he had left into one tremendous
outward sweep of his arm, rather as if he flung a great wing
sideways. He felt his enemy give before it and heard the crash
that marked the collapse of an unstable balance. His own
balance was barely maintained, but his hand in its swift return
touched the hair of the woman's head, and caught it and
fiercely pulled and wrenched till the clasping arms released
their hold and for a moment his body was free. In that
moment he came to his feet, and lightly as some wheeling bird
turned and poised for any new attack. But his enemies lay
still, their shining eyes fixed upon him, their hands scrabbling
on the floor. The hissing and snarling which all this while had
been in his ears ceased gradually; he became aware, as he
stepped watchfully backward, of the sedate room in which that
horrible struggle had gone on. He took another cautious step
away, and bumped into the chair on which he had been sitting,
and the jerk restored him to his ordinary self. He looked, and
saw Miss Wilmot sitting, half-coiled up, on a rug, and Mr.
Foster, her visitor, on one knee near to her, as if he were about
to pick up a book that lay not far off. With alert eyes on them
Anthony suddenly swooped and lifted it. He remembered what
it was without looking.

"I was wrong," he said aloud, and smiling, "it's perfectly
up-to-date. So sorry to be a nuisance, but I still stick to my
own hypothesis. You might think it over. Goodnight, Miss
Wilmot, I'll see myself out. Goodnight, Foster, give my love
to the lion."

He backed carefully to the door, opened it, slipped through,
and found the maid hovering in the little hall. She gazed at
him doubtfully, and he, still rather watchfully, looked back.
Then he saw her expression change into entire amazement and
remembered his collar.

"O sir!" she exclaimed.

"Quite," Anthony said. "But Ephesus, you know——"

"Ephesus, sir?" she asked, more doubtfully still, as he laid his hand on the door.

"My dear," he said, "I'm sorry I can't give you the reference, but your mistress will. It was where St. Paul had trouble with the wild beasts. Go and ask her. Goodnight."

Chapter Eight

MARCELLUS VICTORINUS OF BOLOGNA

In the street he hesitated. He had more or less recovered himself after the struggle, but he felt very strongly that he wasn't ready for any more of the same kind. Suppose Richardson set about him too? On the other hand he had liked Richardson's looks and he was anxious to gather *some* information. So far, what he had was emotional rather than intelligible. He didn't quite see why he should be feeling so cheerful now, but he was. He looked back at those two squatting on the floor not merely with the satisfaction of victory but with an irrational delight that found an additional glee in the small efforts he made to arrange his collar and settle his clothing. The back of his neck was smarting, and his sides were as sore as if a much greater strength than of a mature but small and slight woman had attacked him. But these things did not disturb him. He looked up and down the street and came to a quick decision.

"Come," he said, "let us go and see Mr. Richardson. Perhaps he'll turn into a centipede or a ladybird. Like the princess in the *Arabian Nights*. Let's hope I shall remember to tread on him if he does, though if it's anything like the butterfly I shall be simply too terrified to do anything but scramble on to a chair. I wish I could understand something of what's happening. So I do. Is this the right turning? Apparently. But what will be the end of it all?"

Defeated by this question, he was still staring at it as he came to 17 Bypath Villas. Richardson himself opened the door and took him into a kind of study, where he provided chairs, drinks, and cigarettes. Then he stood back and surveyed his visitor. Anthony spoke however before any question could be asked.

"I have", he said, "been calling on Miss Wilmot. With her Mr. Foster."

Richardson looked at him thoughtfully. "Have you though?" he said. "Which of them was responsible for the collar?"

"Foster," Anthony answered. "Miss Wilmot merely tried to squeeze me to death. It was a very pretty five minutes, if it was real. My body tells me it was, but my mind still rebels; what there is left to rebel."

"I've often wondered whether something of that sort mightn't happen", the other said, "if we got where we were supposed to be going. However. . . What did you want to ask me?"

Their friendly eyes met, and Anthony smiled a little. Then he again ran over his experiences of the past few days, but this time with more conviction. He had been driven into some kind of action, and now he spoke with the certainty that action gives, expecting yet more action and determined to shape it to his will. Richardson heard him to the end without interruption. Then——

"I suspected something of this on Wednesday night," he said sharply. "I suspected it again when I met Foster in the town this afternoon. But I couldn't see how it had begun. Now it's all clear. You're quite right about that, of course."

"But why should they attack *me*?" Anthony asked. "Or why should whatever's in them attack me?"

"I've known them for some time," Richardson answered, "and though it isn't my business to have more opinions than I can help about other people, still I couldn't help seeing something. They were opposite types—Foster was a strong type and Miss Wilmot a weak. But each of them wanted strength and more strength. I've seen Foster frown when anyone contradicted him, and I've seen Miss Wilmot look at her friend when *she* overruled her, and there wasn't much meekness in either of them. They wanted to get as far as they could all right, but I doubt if it was really to contemplate the principles of life. It was much more likely unconsciously to be in order to use the principles of life."

"Meekness," Anthony said meditatively. "I don't know that I feel very meek myself at present. Ought I?"

"You won't get very much safety out of this effort of yours if you go prancing about trying to beat these things by yourself," Richardson answered sardonically. "My good man, what notice do you suppose any of them are going to take of—I don't know your name."

Anthony told him. "But look here," he said, "you're contradicting yourself. If they took notice of Foster, why shouldn't they of me?"

"I don't think they *are* taking much notice of him," answered the other. "His wishes just happen to fit in with their nature. But presently their nature will overwhelm his wishes. Then we shall see. I should imagine there wouldn't be much of Foster left."

"Well, what ought one to do? What do you want to do?" Anthony asked.

Richardson leaned forward and picked up from the table a very old bound book and a very fat exercise book. He again settled himself in his chair, and said, looking firmly at Anthony —"This is the *De Angelis* of Marcellus Victorinus of Bologna, published in the year 1514 at Paris, and dedicated to Leo X."

"Is it?" Anthony said uncertainly.

"Berringer picked it up in Berlin—it's not complete, unfortunately—and lent it to me when he found I was interested to have a shot at translating. There's nothing to show who our Marcellus was, and the book itself, from what he says in .the dedication, isn't so much his own as a version of a work by a Greek—Alexander someone—written centuries before 'in the time of Your Holiness's august predecessor, Innocent the

Second.' In the eleven hundreds about the time of Abelard. However, that doesn't matter. What is interesting is that it seems to confirm the idea that there was another view of angels from that ordinarily accepted. Not very orthodox perhaps, but I suppose orthodoxy wasn't the first requisite at the Court of Leo."

He paused and turned the pages. "I think I'll read you a few extracts," he said. "Most of the dedication is missing; the rest is the usual magniloquence——

" 'For it may rightly be said that Your Holiness both roars as a lion and rides as an eagle, burdens as an ox, and governs as a man, all in defence of the Apostolic and Roman Church: in this singularly uniting the qualities of those great angels, so that Your Holiness is justly'—his adverbs are all over the place—'to be called the Angel of the Church.' Well, we can miss that; probably Leo did. The beginning of the text is missing, but on page 17 we get down to it. You'll have to excuse the English; it amused me to do it in a kind of rhetoric—the Latin suggests it.

" 'These orders then we have received from antiquity, and according to the vision of seers, who nevertheless reserved something from us, that by the devotion of our hearts and the study of the Sacred Word we might ourselves follow in their footsteps and enlarge the knowledge of those secret things which are laid up in heaven. For by such means the Master in Byzantion'—that's the Greek, of course—'expounded to us certain of the symbols and shapes whereby the Divine Celestials are expressed, but partly in riddles lest evil men work sorcery, not certainly upon those Celestials themselves—for how should the propinquity of the Serene Majesty be subject to such hellish markings and invocations?—but upon that appearance of them which, being separated from the Beatific Vision, is dragon-like flung forth into the void. As it is written: *Michael and his angels fought against the dragon and his angels, and the dragon was cast out.* Which is falsely apprehended by many of the profane vulgar, or indeed not at all, for they . . .' "

"Half a second," said Anthony. "I've a feeling for the profane vulgar. What *is* he talking about?"

" 'they', " Richardson read rapidly, " 'suppose that the said dragon is himself a creation and manifest existence, and not rather the power of the Divine Ones arrogated to themselves for sinful purpose by violent men. Now this dragon which is the power of the lion is accompanied also by a ninefold order of spectres, according to the hierarchy of the composed wonders of heaven.' "

"The what?" Anthony exclaimed.

" 'The composed wonders of heaven,' " Richardson repeated; " 'and these spectres being invoked have power upon those who adore them and transform them into their very terrible likeness, destroying them with great moanings; as they do also such as inadvisedly set themselves in the way of such powers, wandering without guide or intelligential knowledge, and being made the prey of the uncontrolled emanations.' "

"Do stop a moment," Anthony said. "Who *are* the uncontrolled emanations?"

Richardson looked up. "The idea seems to be that the energies of these orders can exist in separation from the intelligence which is in them in heaven; and that if deliberately or accidentally you invoke the energy without the intelligence, you're likely eventually to be pretty considerably done for."

"O!" said Anthony. "And the orders are the original Dionysian nine?"

"Right," Richardson agreed. "Well, the next few pages are mostly cursing, and the next few are about the devotion of the Eastern doctor who found it all out. Then we get a little aesthetic theory. 'For albeit those who paint upon parchment or in churches or make mosaic work of precious metals have designed these holy Universals in human shape, presenting them as youths of beautiful appearance, clothed in candid vestures, and this for the indoctrination of the vulgar, who are thereby more easily brought to a humble admiration of such essence and dare to invoke them worthily under the protection of the Blessed Triune, yet it is not to be held by the wise that such human masculinities are in any way even a convenient signification of their true nature; nay, these presentations do in some sense darken the true seeker and communicate confusion, and were it not written that we should have respect to the eyes of children and cast no stone of offence in the way of little ones, it would have been better that such errors should have been forbidden by the wisdom of the Church. For what can the painting of a youth show of those Celestial Benedictions, of which the first circle is that of a lion, and the second circle is that of a serpent, and the third circle is——'

"The next eight pages are missing."

"Damn!" Anthony said heartily. "Doesn't he tell you anywhere else?"

"He doesn't," Richardson said. "When we pick him up he has got right on to the ninth circle which is that of goodness only knows what and is attributed to the seraphim, and he dithyrambs on about the seraphim without giving any clear view of what they are or what they do or how one knows them. Then he quotes many texts about angels in general and becomes almost pious: the sort of thing that Erasmus might have thrown in to placate his enemies the monks. But there's a bit soon after which may interest you—here we are—'written in the Apocalypse. For though these nine zones are divided into a trinity of trinities, yet after another fashion there are four without and four within, and between them is the Glory of the Eagle. For this is he who knows both himself and the others, and is their own knowledge: as it is written *We shall know as are known*—this is the knowledge of the Heavenly Ones in the place of the Heavenly Ones, and it is called the Virtue of the Celestials.' "

He stopped and looked at Anthony. "Tell me again," he said, "how did you seem to escape from the shape this afternoon?"

Marcellus Victorinus of Bologna

"As if I were in an aeropl—— O but . . ." Anthony stopped.
Richardson went on reading——

" 'As it is written *The Lord brought you out of Egypt on the back
of a strong eagle*. And *To the woman were given two wings of a great
eagle*.' That", he added, "is what Marcellus Victorinus of
Bologna thought was the key to the situation." He shut the
books and put them down. After a moment he added: "Not
that that's really all," and picked them up again.

"No," said Anthony, "don't. Tell me yourself—it'll be
simpler for me, and I want to understand."

"I can't possibly tell you," Richardson said, "because I don't
understand it myself. Here we are—'But also the Master hid
from his pupils certain things concerning the shapes and manifestations of the Celsitudes, and spoke secretly of them. For it
is said that he instructed his children in the Lord how that the
knowledge of them was of different kinds, and that the days of
their creation within this earth were three—that is to say, the
fifth, the sixth and the seventh. And the times in which we
now live are the sixth, when man has dominion over the
apparitions of the Divine Universals, but there was a time
before that when man was but dust in their path, so awful
and so fierce were they. As it is written: *let him have dominion*
but not *he has it*, and if any have no such dominion and yet
seek them out he shall behold them unsubdued, aboriginal,
very terrible. But the third day is the Sabbath of the Lord God,
and all things have rest.' " Finally, Richardson went on, "this
is his colophon—'All these thing here have I, Marcellus Victorinus, clerk, of the University of Bologna, gathered out of the
writings which remain of all that was taught by Alexander of
Byzantion, concerning the Holy Angels, their qualities and
appearances. And I invoke the power and authority of the
Sacred Eagle, beseeching him to cover me with his wings in the
time of danger and to bear me upon his wings with joy in the
place of the Heavenly Ones, and to show me the balance of all
things within the gates of Justice; and I offer prayer to him for

all who shall read this book, beseeching them in their turn also to offer prayer for me.' "

"And how", said Anthony after a long pause, "does one set about finding the Sacred Eagle?"

Richardson said nothing, and after another pause Anthony went on: "Besides, if this fellow were right, what harm would the Divine Universals do us? I mean, aren't the angels supposed to be rather gentle and helpful and all that?"

"You're doing what Marcellus warned you against," Richardson said, "judging them by English pictures. All nightgowns and body and a kind of flacculent sweetness. As in cemeteries, with broken bits of marble. These are Angels—not a bit the same thing. These are the principles of the tiger and the volcano and the flaming suns of space."

"Yes," Anthony said, "I see. Yes. Well, to go back, what does one do about it?"

Richardson shrugged his shoulders. "I've done all I can," he uttered, in a more remote voice. "I've told you what Marcellus said, what he thought was the only safe method of dealing with them. Myself, I think he was right."

Anthony felt a sudden collapse threaten him. He leaned back in his chair; exhaustion seized on his body, and helplessness on his mind. Belief, against which he had been unconsciously struggling for days, flooded in upon him, as the sense of a great catastrophe will overtake a man who has endured it without realizing it. It was true then—the earth, the world, pleasant, or unpleasant, accustomed joys, habitual troubles, was the world no longer. They, this room in which he sat, the people he knew, were all on the point of passing under a new and overwhelming dominion; change was threatening them. He thought of Tighe on his knees before his butterflies; he thought of Foster crouched back like a wild animal, and Dora Wilmot's arm twisting like a serpent under his foot; and beyond them he saw in a cloud of rushing darkness the forms of terror that ruled this new creation—the lion, the soaring butterfly, the shaking ripples of the earth that were themselves the serpent. They grew before his blinded eyes moving to a kind of super-natural measure, dancing in space, intertwining on their unknown passages. And then mightier than all, sweeping down towards him, vast wings outspread, fierce beak lowered, he saw the eagle. It passed through those other forms, and came driving directly down. They still moved in a giant pattern behind it, and then it seemed to sweep them forward within its wings. It came rushing at him; he felt his lower jaw beginning to jerk uncontrollably; his eyes were shut; his heart was swelling till it must, it must, break; he was leaning sideways over his chair. But in that moment he forced himself upright; he forced open his eyes, and saw Richardson leaning against the mantelpiece and the book of Marcellus Victorinus on the table.

"The place, I think," Richardson was saying, "is in Berringer's house. You either go or you don't; you either invoke or you don't; you either rule or you don't. But certainly in this present dispensation even the angelic universals were given to the authority of men. So far as man chooses. There is another way."

Chapter Nine

THE FUGITIVE

Damaris had gone out for a walk, not that she wanted to, but because, as she had rather definitely told her father, it seemed the only way of getting a little peace. In general Damaris associated peace with her study, her books, and her manuscripts rather than with the sky, the hills, and the country roads; and not unjustly, since only a few devout followers of Wordsworth can in fact find more than mere quiet in the country. The absence of noise is not in all cases the same thing as the presence of peace. Wordsworth also found morality there, and no-one is ever likely to find peace without morality of one sort or another. But Damaris had never yet received any kind of impulse from either vernal or autumnal woods to teach her more of moral evil and of good than all her sages. Certainly she had found no particular impulse that way in her sages either, but that was because she was rapidly becoming incapable of recognizing a moral impulse when she saw it, the sages from Pythagoras onwards meaning something quite different from her collocation. Peace to her was not a state to be achieved but a supposed necessary condition of her daily work, and peace therefore, as often happens, evaded her continually. She ingeminated *Peace* so often and so loudly that she inevitably frightened it still farther away, peace itself being (so far as has yet been found) a loveliness only invocable by a kind of sympathetic magic and auto-hypnotism which it never occurred to her to exercise. In a convulsive patience therefore she walked firmly out of the town, and up the rising ground that lay about it.

The Fugitive

For the last day or two the centre of gravity of her world seemed slightly to have shifted. This had begun when she had found the attention of her audience diverted on the Wednesday evening, but it had become more marked with Mr. Foster's call on Thursday, and had really shocked her with Anthony's that Saturday morning. Except that it was silly, she would almost have supposed that those two gentlemen had found her father's odd antics more important than her own conversation. They seemed to be looking past her, at some other fact on their horizon; they were preoccupied, they diffused neglect. Her father too—he had been almost patronizing once or twice, infinitely and unconsciously superior. She was liable to find him anywhere about the house or garden—doing nothing, saying nothing, looking nothing; if she spoke to him, which she often did out of mere irritable good nature, he took a moment to collect himself before he replied. She would have been prepared to make allowances for this if he had been engaged upon his butterflies—having at least an understanding of how hobbies affected people, though this particular hobby seemed to her more silly than many. But he wasn't; he just sat or stood about. It was all very well for Mr. Foster to be so profoundly interested—Mr. Foster didn't have to live with him. As for Anthony——

She walked a little faster. Anthony's call had been at a stupid time to begin with, but its purpose—which really did seem to have been to see her father—made it wholly stupid in itself. What *could* Anthony at half-past eleven on Saturday morning want with her father? It annoyed her that she had to take a little care in dealing with Anthony—he was so persistently attached and yet at the same time apt to become troublesomely detached. She disliked the slight feeling of anxiety she had about him—of late she found herself occasionally wondering after each visit whether, when he had gone, he had gone for good. And there was at present simply no other convenient way of getting some of her articles into print. They were good articles of their kind—she and Anthony both knew that—only there weren't very many papers that would care for them. And it did—she half angrily admitted—it did help her, please, encourage, whatever the right word was, to see her name printed at the top of a column. It was a mark and reward of work done and a promise of work and reward to be. It was, in short, an objectivization of Miss Tighe to a point elsewhere at present unobtainable. Probably, though she did not think of this, Abelard, *mutatis mutandis*, felt a similar satisfaction at his lectures, with perhaps less danger owing to the watch that his confessor would have expected Abelard to keep over his conscience.

However, here she was away from them, and a good thing too. For this business of the relation of the Divine Perfection with creation was giving her, as it had given the schoolmen, a little trouble. Plato's Absolute Beauty, she quite saw, was all right because that was not necessarily conscious of the world; but the God of Abelard *was* conscious of the world, and yet that consciousness must not be necessary to Him, for nothing but Himself could be necessary to Him. St. Thomas—only he was later; she didn't want to bring him in, still a short appendix perhaps, bringing the history of the idea up to St. Thomas . . . just to show that she had read well beyond her subject. . . . St. Thomas would be a good stopping-place, and she might reasonably not pursue it further. Perhaps the whole thing had better be in an appendix—*On the Knowledge of the World* . . . no, on *God's Idea of the World from Plato to Aquinas*. Something was wrong with that title, she thought vaguely, but she could alter it presently. The main thing at the moment was to get clear in her mind the various methods by which God was said to know the world. Joyn the Scot had taught that the account of the Creation in Genesis—"let the earth bring forth the living creature after his kind"—referred, not to the making of the earthly animals, but to the formation of the kinds and orders in the Divine Mind before they took on visible and material shapes. Well, now . . .

acquainted: the long wrangles of the early scholastics about universals, a sentence or two from Augustine, a statement from Porphyry . . . it was Quentin Sabot who uttered them. A couple of lines from one of Abelard's own hymns especially rang in her ears as such things will.

> *Est in re veritas*
> *Jam non in schemate;*

until her maddened mind produced (incorrectly) as a translation:

> *Truth is always in the thing;*
> *never in the reasoning.*

Quentin's face went on looking at her and repeating this couplet until she could have cried with weariness and misery.

For she was miserable; also she was afraid. She wasn't—no, she certainly wasn't Anthony's girl, but he was Anthony's friend. And if her relations with Anthony had any truth at all, then she was committed to at least such an amount of care for Anthony's wishes as he would have given to hers. For any mightier gift, for any understanding of that state in which she might profoundly and nobly love merely because opportunity for love was offered, she was not asked. She had taken—she knew she had taken—and she had, even by that measure, failed. She produced excuses, reasons, apologies even, and then as she argued there was that distracted face again, and from the distracted mouth came the singing doggerel:

> *Truth is always in the thing;*
> *never in the . . .*

Est in re veritas—but that was all about religion and metaphysics; it was from a hymn for Lauds on Sunday. What had it to do with Quentin Sabot in a ditch? Anthony would be angry with her? Anthony had no right . . . Anthony couldn't expect . . . Anthony oughtn't to demand. . . . All that was very well, but she realized that it hadn't much to do with Anthony. He might not demand or expect or claim, but he would undoubtedly *be*. *Est in re veritas*—O damn, damn!

She ought to be superior to all that. What was the phrase in the *Phaedrus?*—"the soul of the philosopher alone has wings." She ought to be rising above . . . above helping anyone in a ditch, above speaking in goodwill to the friend of her friend, above trying to bring peace to the face that now pursued her.— No, she ought, in fairness to Anthony, to have done something. "I was wrong," she said, almost irritably, and with a fierce determination not to admit it to Anthony.

She met him therefore when the next morning—Sunday morning of all times—he appeared again, with a destructive fire. As he had been preparing every kind of flag of truce as he came along, under cover of which his diplomacy was to attempt her removal to London, this at first threw him into complete disorder, more especially as he could not for the moment understand what had provoked this fresh battle. She was asking, he at last made out, why he didn't look after his friend better, and at that he broke through her talk.

"Have you seen him then?" he asked sharply. "Where? when? No, don't chatter; tell me."

Damaris told him—in general terms. "It was an extraordinarily unpleasant time," she said. "I do think, Anthony, you oughtn't to have let him go off by himself, if that's the state he's in."

Anthony looked at her, and then took a turn through the room. Before his eyes, as he looked, she had seemed to change; the thought of Quentin, cast off, kicked at by her outraged anger, hurt him profoundly, and the sombre eyes with which he surveyed her saw a different and nastier Damaris. Yet he had known it all along—only that she should treat him as she did was part of the joke of things, that she should treat Quentin so seemed somehow so much worse. But of course it wasn't worse; it was the same Damaris. Those whom he loved were at war. But Love itself wasn't and couldn't be at war. He loved her, and she had persecuted his friend. But he loved them both, and therefore there was no taking of sides. Love itself never could take sides. His heart ached in him, but as he came back to her his eyes were smiling, even though his face had been struck by pain.

"*O quanta qualia*," he murmured, pausing near her. "Those something sabbaths the blessed ones see. Dearest, you'll be like the fellow in the New Testament; you'll meet Abelard one day and he'll stare at you and say he never knew you. I suppose you know you've been a pig."

"Don't talk to me like that," Damaris said, and in the contention of emotions within her added absurdly, "It was a great shock to me."

"You've got a worse shock than that coming to you," he answered.

"Why do you always talk as if I didn't know anything?" she asked, opening another attack on more favourable ground; and added, to distract him still further, "And then you expect me to marry you."

"I don't expect anything at all," he said, "not from anybody. Least of all from you. If you were going to marry me, if you weren't shut up, I should have knocked your damn silly head off your shoulders. But as it is—no. Only the sooner you leave off expecting the better you're likely to be. Will you come to London?"

Damaris almost gaped, the question was so sudden, "Will I —will I what?" she exclaimed. "Why on earth should I go to London?"

"Quentin—God's mercy save him now!—offered you a hole in a ditch . . . I offer you London," Anthony said. "The reason is that the princes of heaven are in the world and you're not used to them. No, stop a minute, and let me tell you. In your own language, you owe me that."

He paused to choose his words. "Something has driven Quentin into panic and hiding; something has turned your father away from his hobby to inaction and contemplation; something frightened you all at Berringer's house the other night; something has obsessed Foster and your friend Miss Wilmot till they attacked me yesterday evening; yes, they did —I am not mad, most noble Festa; something is sounding in the world like thunder——"

"Attacked you! What nonsense!" Damaris cried.

"—and you can stop and meet it if you choose. Or you can come to London for a few days' grace at least."

"If this is a joke——" she began.

"If it is," he answered, "all your philosophers and schoolmen were mad together. And your life's work is no more than the comparison of different scribblings in the cells of a lunatic asylum."

She stood up, staring at him. "If this is your way of getting back on me", she said, "because I didn't do what you think I ought to for your insane friend——"

"What I think is of no matter," he answered. "Have I pretended it was? It's the thing that matters: the truth is in the thing. Heart's dearest, listen—the things you study are true, and the philosophers you read knew it. The universals are abroad in the world, and what are you going to do about it? Besides write about them."

"Do you seriously mean to tell me", she said, "that Power is walking about on the earth? Just Power?"

"Yes," he answered, and though she added before she could stop herself, "Don't you even know what a philosophic universal is?" he said no more. For his energy sank within, carrying her, presenting, agonizing for her, holding the Divine Eagle by the wings that its perfect balance might redeem them, holding both her and Quentin and his own thought that they all might

The Fugitive

live together in the strong and lovely knowledge which was philosophy. So that he did not notice at first that she was saying coldly, "Perhaps you'd better go now."

When this penetrated his mind, he made a last effort. "But the things I just spoke of—at least they're true," he said. "Your father *has* given up butterflies; you *were* startled; Quentin *has* been driven almost mad. What do you suppose did it? Come away for a day or two—just till we can find out. Ah do! If"— he hesitated—"if you"—he compelled himself to go on—"if you owe me anything, do this to please me."

Damaris paused. She did not know that one of the crises of her life had arrived, nor did she recognize in its full deceptiveness the temptation that rose in her. But she paused uncertain whether to pretend that in effect she did not owe him anything, or to admit that she did. On the very point of taking hypocritical refuge she paused, and merely answered instead: "I don't see any reason to go to London, thank you." She was to see that cold angry phrase as the beginning of her salvation.

He shrugged and was silent. He couldn't go on appealing; he could not yet compel. He couldn't think of anything more to do or say, yet he hated to leave her. He wondered what Marcellus Victorinus would have done in this quandary. Rockbotham would be expecting him soon. . . .

Well, that way was the only one that lay open; he would take that way. He couldn't quite see what was to be gained by looking at the adept, but that possibility—and no other—had been presented to him. He would go. He gave his hand to Damaris.

"Goodbye, then," he said. "Don't be too angry with me—not for a week, anyhow. After that. . . ."

"I don't understand you a bit," she said, and then made a handsome concession—after all, she *did* owe him something, and he *was* upset over Quentin—"but I think you're trying to be kind. . . . I'm sorry about your friend—perhaps if it hadn't been so sudden. . . . You see, I was pre-occupied with that bothering business of the Divine Perfection. . . . Anthony, you're hurting my hand!"

"I understand that it can be a trouble," he said. "O Almighty Christ! Goodbye. We may meet at Philippi yet."

And then he went.

Chapter Ten

THE PIT IN THE HOUSE

The conversation between Anthony and Dr. Rockbotham in the car on the way to Berringer's house was of the politest and chattiest kind, interspersed with moments of seriousness. They began by discussing the curious meteorological conditions, agreeing that such frequent repetitions of thunder without lightning or rain were very unusual.

"Some kind of electrical nucleus, I suppose," the doctor said, "though why the discharge should be audible but not visible, I don't know."

"I noticed it when I was down on Thursday," Anthony remarked, "and again yesterday. It seems to be louder when we get out of town; inside it's much less."

"Deadened by the ordinary noises, I expect," the doctor said. "Very upsetting for some of my patients—the nervous ones, you know. Even quite steady people are affected in the funniest way sometimes. Now my wife, for instance—nobody less nervous than she is, you'll agree—yet when she came in this morning—there's an old servant of ours she generally calls on every Sunday morning when it's fine and she's not busy—she had an extraordinary tale of a kind of small earthquake."

"Earthquake!" Anthony exclaimed.

"She declared the ground shifted under her," the doctor went on. "She was crossing the allotments just round by the railway bridge at the time, and she nearly fell on a lot of cabbages; in fact she did stumble among them—rather hurt her foot, which was how it cropped up. Of course I wouldn't say there couldn't have been a slight shock, but I was about the

109

town at the time, and I didn't notice anything. You didn't either, I suppose?"

"Nothing at all," Anthony said.

"No, I thought not," the doctor said. "The heat too—do you feel it? It's going to be a very trying summer."

Anthony, lying back in the car, with a grim look on his face, said, "It is going to be a very trying summer."

"You don't like this heat?" the doctor asked. And "I don't like *this* heat," Anthony with perfect truth replied.

"Well, we don't all of us. I don't mind it myself," the doctor said. "It's the winter I don't care for. A doctor's life, you know; all sorts of weather and all sorts of people. Especially the people; I sometimes say I'd as soon be doctor to a zoo."

"Talking of zoos, did they ever catch the lioness that got loose round here the other day?" Anthony asked.

"Now that was a funny thing," the other answered. "We heard all sorts of rumours on the Tuesday night, but there's been no more news. They think it must have gone in the other direction and they've been following it that way, I believe. Of course people are a bit shy of coming out of the town by night, but that's sheer funk. These imprisoned creatures are very timorous, you know. Supposing there ever *was* a lioness at all. The show itself moved on the next day, and when I saw the Chief Inspector on Friday he was inclined to laugh at the idea."

"Was he?" Anthony said. "He must be a brave man."

"As I said to him," the doctor went on, "I'd rather laugh at the idea than the thing. So would anybody, I expect."

He paused, but Anthony had no wish to answer. He felt a constriction at his heart as he listened; "the idea" meant to him a spasm of fear, and he was aware that he existed unhappily between two states of knowledge, between the world around him, the pleasant ordinary world in which one laughed at or discussed ideas, and a looming unseen world where ideas—or something, something living and terrible, passed on its own business, overthrowing minds, wrecking lives, and scattering destruction as it went. There already was the house, silent and secret, in which perhaps potentialities beyond all knowledge waited or shaped themselves. Need he get out of the car—as he was doing? open the gate—enter the garden? Couldn't he get back now, on some excuse or none, before the door opened and they had to go in to where that old man, as he remembered him, lay in his terrible passivity? What new monstrosity, what beast of indescribable might or beauty, was even now perhaps dragging itself down the stairs? What behemoth would come lumbering through the hall?

Actually the only behemoth, and though she was fat she was hardly that, was the housekeeper. She let them in, she conversed with the doctor; she ushered them up the stair to where at the top the male nurse waited. Anthony followed, and, his heart full of Quentin and Damaris, aspired to the knowledge which should give them both security and peace. He remembered the sentences over which he had brooded half the night. "The first circle is of the lion; the second circle is of the serpent; the third circle——" O what, what was the third? what sinister fate centuries ago had so mutilated that volume of angelical lore as to forbid his discovery now? "The wings of an eagle"— well, if that was what was needed, then, so far as he could, he would enter into that circle of the eagle which was the—what had the sentence said?—"The knowledge of the Celestials in the place of the Celestials."

"And God help us all," he added to himself, as he came into the bedroom.

He stood aside while the doctor, leaning over the bed, made his examination. There had, the nurse's report told them, been no change; still silent and motionless the adept lay before them. Anthony walked over to the bed while the doctor spoke to the nurse, and looked at the body. The eyes were open but unseeing; he gazed into them, and went on gazing. Here perhaps, could he reach it, the secret lay; he leaned closer, seeking, half-unconsciously, to penetrate it. For a moment he could have fancied that they flicked into life, but not common life; that a dangerous vitality threatened him. Threaten? he leaned nearer again—"the knowledge of the Celestials in the place of the Celestials." Quentin—Damaris. He could not avoid the challenge that had momently gleamed from those eyes; it had vanished, but he intensely expected its return. He forgot the doctor; he forgot Berringer; he forgot everything but those open unresponsive eyes in which lurked the presage of defeat or victory. What moved, what gleamed, what shone at him there? What was opening?

"Quite comatose, poor fellow!" a voice close by him gibbered suddenly.

"Er—yes," said Anthony, and pulled himself upright. He could have sworn that the slightest film passed over the eyes, and reluctantly he turned his own away. But they were dazzled with the strain; he could not see the room very clearly; there seemed to be dark openings everywhere—the top of the jug on the wash stand, the mirror of the dressing-table, the black handle of the grey painted door, all these were holes in things, entrances and exits perhaps, like rabbit holes in a bank from which something might rapidly issue. He heard the dull voice say again: "Shall we go downstairs?" and found himself walking cautiously across the room. As he came near the door he couldn't resist a backward glance—and the head had turned surely, and the eyes were watching him? No—it was still quiet on the pillow, but over beyond it the dressing-table mirror showed an oval blackness. He looked at it steadily, then he became aware that he was standing by the door right in the doctor's way; with a murmur of apology he seized the handle and opened it.

"It makes it so awkward," Dr. Rockbotham said, passing through, with a little bow of acknowledgement, "when there is no easy way of——"

Anthony followed, shutting the door after him, and as he turned to step along the landing, found that he stood on a landing indeed but no more that of the simple house into which he had so recently come. It was a ledge rather than a landing, and though below him he saw the shadowy forms of staircase and hall, yet below him and below these there fell great cliffs, bottomless, or having the bottom hidden by flooding darkness. He was standing above a vast pit, the walls of which swept away from him on either side till they closed again opposite him, and some sort of huge circle was complete. He looked down with—he was vaguely aware—a surprising freedom from fear; and presently he turned his eyes upward, half-expecting to see that same great wall extending incalculably high above his head. So indeed it did, but there was a difference, for above it leaned outward, and far away he saw a cloudy white circle of what seemed the sky. He would have known it for the sky only that it was in motion; it was continually passing into the wall of the abyss, so that a pale vibration was for ever surging in and around and down those cliffs, as if a steady landside slipped ever downwards in waves of movement, which at last were lost to sight somewhere in the darkness below. He half put his hand out to touch the wall behind him and then desisted, for such effort would assuredly be vain. It was to the distance and the space that his attention was invited—more, he began to feel, than his attention, even his will and his action. The persistent faint shadow of the staircase distracted him; it hung on the side of the pit and the hall to which it led seemed to be part of the cliff. But he didn't want to look at that—his awaking concentration passed deeper, expecting something, waiting for something, perhaps that wind which he felt beginning to blow. It was very gentle at first, and it was blowing round him and outwards, forcing him, as it grew stronger, towards the brink of the ledge. There came upon him an impulse to resist, to press back, to cling to his footing on this tiny break in the smooth sweep of the cliff, to preserve himself in his own niche of safety. But as still that strength increased he would yield to such a desire; a greater thing than that was possible—

it was for him to know, urgently for him to know, what that other thing might be. He was standing on the very edge, and the wind was rising into driving might, and a dizziness caught him; he could not resist—why then, to yield, to throw himself outward on the strength that was driving through him as well as around him, to be one with that power, to be blown on it and yet to be part of it—nothing could oppose or bear up against it and him in it. Yet on the edge he pressed himself back; not so, was his passage to be achieved—it was for him to rise above that strength of wind; whether he went down or up it must be by great volition, and it was for such volition that he sought within him. But as he steadied himself there slid a doubt into his mind; what and how could he will? He was thinking faster than he had ever done, and questions rose out of nothing and followed each other—what was *to will*? Will was determination to choose—what was choice? How could there be choice, unless there was preference, and if there was preference there was no choice, for it was not possible to choose against that preferring nature which was his being; yet being consisted in choice, for only by taking and doing this and not that could being know itself, could it indeed be; to be then consisted precisely in making an inevitable choice, and all that was left was to know the choice, yet even then was the chosen thing the same as the nature that chose, and if not . . . So swiftly the questions followed each other that he seemed to be standing in flashing coils of subtlety, an infinite ring of vivid intellect and more than intellect, for these questions were not of the mind alone but absorbed into themselves physical passion and twined through all his nature on an unceasing and serpentine journey.

And still all round the walls of the abyss that shaking landslide went on, veiling the dark background with waves of moving pallor within it, and faint colour grew in dark and light, and immense ripples shook themselves down or up, and swifter and swifter those coils of enormous movement went by. By a violent action of the will he questioned Anthony again, drew himself back both from safety and from abandonment, and paused in expectation of what new danger should arise.

His eyes went upward and beheld the sky, and against that sky, as if descending from an immense distance within it, came a winged form. High at first and lifted up, it came down in lessening spirals, until it hovered in mid-air opposite him, and then drove towards the other side of the abyss, and came round again, and hovered, facing him. It was a giant of the eagle kind; and its eyes, even from that remote distance, burned at him with so piercing a gaze that he shut his own and stepped back against the wall behind him. He had heard of drowning men who had seen their whole life in the instant before death, and in a like simultaneous presentation he was aware of his own: of innumerable actions—many foolish, some evil; many beautiful, some holy. And as if he read the history of another soul he saw running through all the passionate desire for intellectual and spiritual truth and honesty, saw it often blinded and thwarted, often denied and outraged, but always it rose again and soared in his spirit, itself like an eagle, and always he followed in it the way that it and he had gone together. The sight of his denials burned through him: his whole being grew one fiery shame, and while he endured to know even this because things were so and not otherwise, because to refuse to know himself as he was would have been a final outrage, a last attempt at flight from the Power that challenged him and in consequence an entire destruction by it—while he endured the fire fell away from him and he himself was mysteriously rushing over the abyss. He was riding in the void, flying without wings, securely existing by movement and balance among the dangers of that other world. He was poised in a vibration of peace, carried within some auguster passage. The myriad passage of the butterflies recurred to his consciousness, and with an inrush of surpassing happiness he knew that he was himself offering himself to the state he had so long desired. Triumphant over the twin guardians of that place of realities, escaped from the lion and the serpent, he grew into his proper office, and felt the flickers of prophecy pass through him, of the things of knowledge that were to be. Borne now between the rush of gigantic wings he went upward and again swept down; and the cliffs of the abyss had vanished, for he moved now amid sudden shapes and looming powers. Patterned upon the darkness he saw the forms—the strength of the lion and the subtlety of the crowned serpent, and the loveliness of the butterfly and the swiftness of the horse—and other shapes whose meaning he did not understand. They were there only as he passed, hints and expressions of lasting things, but not by such mortal types did the Divine Ones exist in their own blessedness. He knew, and submitted; this world was not yet open to him, nor was his service upon earth completed. And as he adored those beautiful, serene, and terrible manifestations, they vanished from around him. He was no more in movement; he was standing again on his ledge; a rush of mighty wings went outward from him, and the darkness of the walls in which it was lost swept towards him on all sides. A noise of hollow echoes came to him, and he was aware of his own limbs making abrupt and jerky movements. He saw a barrier by him, and laid his hand on it in the dizziness that attacked him. This passed and he came to himself.

"—discovering where his relations live—if any," Dr. Rockbotham said, shaking his head, and beginning the descent of the stairs.

"Quite," said Anthony, following him slowly down and into one of the rooms on the ground floor. He wasn't sorry to sit down; the doctor meanwhile wandering round rather restlessly. He was saying something but Anthony was incapable of knowing what, or what his own voice at intervals said in answer. What on earth had happened on the landing? Had he fainted? Surely not or the doctor would have noticed it—people generally did notice when other people fainted. But he felt very breathless, and yet quite keen. Damaris—something or other

was necessary for Damaris. No hurry; it would be clear soon
what he was to do. Quentin too—if Quentin had only held
out, he would be safe yet. And then the end.

Apparently during this settling of his inner faculties he had
been saying the right things, for the doctor was now standing
at the french windows looking quite satisfied.

"Very good," Anthony said, and stood up.

"Yes," Dr. Rockbotham answered, "I think that'll be best.
After all, as things are, there's no immediate hurry."

"None at all," Anthony agreed, and rather wondered why.
It was certain that there wasn't, not for whatever Rockbotham
was talking about; the things about which there was, if not
hurry, at least a necessity for speed, were quite other. But for
a knowledge of them he must wait on the Immortals.

"Well, shall we go?" the doctor said, and they began to
move towards the door. As Anthony stood up however his eyes
caught—he paused to look and it had gone—a sudden point of
flame flickering in a corner of the ceiling. He stepped forward,
his eyes still fixed on the spot, and again he saw a little rapid
tongue of fire burn down the whole corner of the room from
ceiling to floor. It swept down and vanished, and he saw the
wallpaper unsinged behind it. He shifted his gaze, glancing
round the room; as he took in the floor he saw another flame
spring up all round his foot as he put it down, and then that
also was gone. The doctor, just in front of him, was passing
through the doorway, and as he did so a thin line of fire
flamed along doorposts and lintel so that Rockbotham stood for
a moment in an arch of fire; he went on, and it had disappeared. Anthony followed him into the hall; there also as he
went the sudden little flames peered out and vanished—one
curled momently round the unbrella-stand, one spread itself
in a light glow over the lid of a huge chest that stood there, one
broke in a rosy flower of fire right in the middle of the wall and
then folded itself up and faded. Anthony caught up with the
doctor, and opened his lips to speak, but before he could do so a

sudden sharp pain struck into his side, near his heart, as if the beak of a great bird had wounded him. He gasped involuntarily, and the doctor looked round.

"Did you speak?" he asked.

Down the open doorway in front, where the housekeeper was holding the door for them, fell a rain of fiery sparks, and then a curtain of leaping flames, pointing upward and falling downward, as if some burning thing had been dropped. The housekeeper was looking through it at the garden; the pain stabbed again at Anthony's heart. He shook his head with an articulate murmur, as the doctor nodded goodbye to the woman, and as Anthony, silent, followed his example, the sharp injury ceased, and a throb of relief and content took its place. In the virtue of that healing silence he got into the car and sat down.

"The thunder's still sounding," the doctor said as they started.

"Is it?" Anthony said. It did not strike him as particularly curious that he could not hear it, though with a certain amusement he reflected that if the servants of the Immortals were blind and deaf to the sights and sounds ordinary people noticed it might be slightly inconvenient. Perhaps that, in the past, was why so many of them came to violent and painful ends. But the thunder—which was not thunder, he knew, but the utterance of the guardian of the angelical world—he certainly could not hear. He almost felt as if he might if he gave his whole attention to it, but why give his whole attention to it, unless it would please anyone very much? And he didn't think Dr. Rockbotham was interested enough to want that.

During the ride he looked at the country. Things were not yet clear to him; but communication was going on within him. As they ran past the first few scattered houses of the town, he thought he saw once more the shape of the lion, but he noticed it with awe certainly but now with no fear. The strength that had once overthrown him had now no power upon him; he was within it, and under the protection of another of the great Ideas, that Wisdom which knew the rest and itself also, the very tradition of the Ideas and the Angelicals being but a feather dropped from its everlasting and effectual wing.

Dr. Rockbotham said: "Did you happen to try and lift his hand?

"Curious, very curious," the doctor ran on. "It's almost impossible, so heavy, so impossible to move. I've never known a case quite like this. If there's no change to-morrow I shall certainly get another opinion."

How could one move the gate of the universals? pull up the columns through which they passed? But Rockbotham was a good man; he was serving to the best of his power, innocent, devoted, mild, surrendered to the intention of some one of these Authorities which had yet not become manifest. He would go safely among outer wonders until the place of goodness was reached, and then—if that assumption were still proceeding —be gently received into his ruling Idea. Happy were those who found so simple and easy a passing! For others, for those who were given up to the dragon and not to the angel, it might be a more difficult way. From such destruction at least he believed Damaris to be, by her very ignorance and unmalicious childishness, secure.

He refused an invitation to lunch, parted from his companion at the door of his hotel, and after a solitary meal went to his room, and there fell asleep. He slept without disturbance and without dreams till late in the evening, and woke at peace. In the same inner quiet he rose, changed, and set out for Richardson's. What took him there he could hardly tell, and did not indeed trouble to inquire. In that profound sleep something seemed to have been lost; the little goblin of self-consciousness which always, deride it as he would, and derision in fact only nourished and magnified it, danced a saraband in his mind—that goblin had faded and was gone. He moved, though he did not know it, with a new simplicity, and his very walk through the streets had in it a quality of intention which it had never before possessed. He rang in the same way, with no doubt whether Richardson was at home; if Richardson had not been at home he would not have been there, he knew. When he was admitted he shook hands with a joyous smile.

Richardson, when they were settled, sat back and studied him. Anthony, at amused leisure, noticed this and waited for the other to speak.

At last—"You're there then?" Richardson said.

"There?" Anthony asked. "If you mean the house, I've been there."

"Do you know how bright your eyes are?" the other irrelevantly asked.

Anthony broke into a laugh, the first time he had laughed wholeheartedly for several days. "Well, that's jolly!" he said. "I hope they'll impress Damaris that way." But he offered no explanation of the name and Richardson courteously ignored it. Instead, he said, thoughtfully, "So you've been to the house? And what do you know of things now?"

Anthony found himself a little unwilling to speak, not because he mistrusted Richardson, but because to recount his own experience would take them no farther. It was no use saying to another soul, "I did—I saw—I was—this, that, or the other," because what applied to him couldn't apply to anyone else, not to anyone else at all in the whole community of mankind. Some more general, some ceremonial utterance was needed. Now, if ever, he needed the ritual of words arranged and shaped for that end. He saw the *De Angelis* on the table, leaned forward, and picked it up, looking over at Richardson as he did so.

"How can *I* tell you?" he said. "We don't know Victorinus; let's see if he can be the mouthpiece of the gods. Shall I?"

"Do as you like," the other answered. "Perhaps you're

right; if the symbols are there ready why bother to make fresh?"

Anthony considered this for a few seconds, as if it held some meaning of which he was uncertain. But presently he opened the book, and slowly turned the pages, reading aloud a sentence here and there, and translating as he read. To a certain extent he had always kept up his own Latin, but it was not merely that knowledge which now enabled him to understand so easily the antique habit of the tongue; his perseverance did but open the way to a larger certainty.

" 'As it is written *Where wast thou when I laid the foundations of the world?* and this is the place of the foundations, out of which there arise all kinds of men compact of powers; and therefore it was that when the Lord would rebuke Job he demanded of him concerning the said foundations, saying *Doth the eagle mount up at thy command?* and *She dwelleth on the crag of the rock and the strong place.* . . .

" 'But the names that are given are of one kind, as when it is said among the wise that there is strength or beauty, or humility, meaning that certain men are strong or beautiful or humble, which certain heretics wrenched to their destruction, saying that these names were no more than words used for many like things and had in themselves no meaning; and the shapes which are seen are of another, as the lion and the eagle and the unicorn and the lamb. . . Nor is either made sufficient, but as a foreknowledge of the revelation that shall be.' . . .

" 'Also they have power in death, and woe unto him that is given up to them and torn aside between them, having no authority over the Mighty Ones because he is cast out from salvation and hath never governed them in himself.' . . .

" 'For there is a mystery of the earth and the air, and of the water and the air, and the Divine Ones manifest themselves in both according to their natures; so that the circle of the lion is that of leviathan, and of the others accordingly: as it is written *There is one flesh of beasts and another of fish*: and *They that go down to the sea in ships these see the works of the Lord and his wonders in the great deep. . . .'* "

Anthony stopped reading, and Richardson said briefly: "But there is something beyond them all."

"It may be," the other said, "and that I suppose we shall discover in time. Meanwhile——"

"There is no meanwhile at all," Richardson interrupted. "I think that this fellow was quite right, and I believe you've seen and known something. But for myself I will go straight to the end."

Anthony swayed the book slowly in his hand. "Isn't there an order", he said, "in everything? If one has to find balance, and a kind of movement in balance . . . I mean, to act here where we are. . . ."

"But I don't want to act where we are," the other cried out sharply. "Why should one act?"

"Other people, perhaps," Anthony almost shyly suggested. "If by any chance . . ."

He stopped abruptly, and listened. Then he stood up, put down the book, and said, "Open the window." The words were not exactly a command nor a request; they came to Richardson rather as a statement of something he was about to do; they passed on into the outer world a thing which was already preordained. But though he moved to obey he was already too late; Anthony had crossed the room, pushed the window up, and was leaning out. Richardson came up behind him and also listened.

The Sunday evening was very quiet. A few noises, wheels, footsteps, a door shutting, broke the stillness, and from some distance off the last hymn of the evening service at some church. That died away, and for a few minutes there was utter silence. In that silence there came to Anthony, distant but shrill, the sound of a woman's terrified scream. He pulled himself back, shut the window, said to Richardson, "I'm sorry, I must go. That was Damaris," and moved with extreme lightness and extreme quickness to the front door, gathering his hat and stick in one movement as he passed. Richardson called out something which he did not catch; he waved his hand, took a leap down the steps, and ran along the street at top speed.

He was happily aware, as he went, of how easy, how lovely, it was to run like this; he was, more deeply and even more happily, aware that the moment for which he had long waited was come. But he was not aware of himself as bringing any help; it was his business to run because by that some sort of help could reach Damaris; what he could no more tell than he could tell what danger had threatened her and had wrung from her that scream which some interior faculty of his soul had caught. He came to the corner and turned it.

Richardson, startled out of his contemplations by Anthony's movement, had at first hesitated, and then, half-involuntarily, followed, as if drawn in the other's train. But when he in turn came to the corner he stopped. He saw Anthony before him but he saw something else too.

In the middle of the street was a horse and cart. Or there had been. It had been jogging along peacefully enough when suddenly its sleeping driver felt the reins torn from his hand, heard a crash and a rending, awoke from his doze, and saw the horse tearing itself free of cart and harness. Its white coat gleamed silver; it grew larger and burst the leather bands that held it; it tossed its head, and the absurd blinkers fell off; it swept its tail round and the shafts snapped and fell. The horse made one final plunge and stood free. The frightened driver, cursing, began to clamber out of the cart. As he did so, he saw a young man running down the street at a tremendous speed, and shouted to him to get hold of the horse's head. The young man swerved, apparently to obey, came up to the horse, leapt with the full force of his run, and with one hand to its neck so sat astride. The driver, half-way between his seat and the ground, cried out again with greater oaths, and fell gapingly silent. For the young man, now settling himself,

turned the horse with his heel, and both against the sinking sun
faced the terrified man. They were, he dimly realized, start-
lingly magnificent; they loomed before him, and then the
horse was in motion and they were both flying down the street.

From the corner Richardson, standing still, watched them
go, seeing, for the first time in this new world of appearances,
the union of high powers for high ends. Where they were going
he could not tell, but they went with glory scattered about
them and the noise of music. There seemed to him, as he
watched, to be not one horse but many horses charging away
from him down the street, herds from the pampas and the
steppes, a thundering army, riotous and untamed. Here and
there amid those tossing manes he saw riders, but their shape
and aspect he could not see, only far beyond that wild expanse
of haunches and backs and necks, he saw Anthony, sitting
easily upright, leading them, directing them, by virtue of the
steed he rode. Down that provincial street all the horses of the
world seemed pouring, but he realized that what he saw was
only the reflection of the single Idea. One form, and only one,
was galloping away from him: these other myriads were its
symbols and exhalations. They were not there, not yet, how
uneasily soever in stables and streets the horses of that neighbourhood stirred and stamped, and already kicked at gates and
carts in order to break free. They were not yet there, although
far away on Eastern and Western plains, the uneasy herds
started, and threw up their heads and snuffled at the air, and
whinnied, and broke into quick charges, feeling already upon
the wind the message of that which they were. 'The huntsmen
in Persia' soothed their steeds; Chinese squadrons on the march
or at bivouac were thrown into disorder; the grooms of the
Son of Heaven in Tokio and Kioto ran in alarm to their
charges. Out on the Pacific other keepers watched anxiously in
scattered ships the restless stamping of sea-borne steeds;
farmers in America left their work, and small Mexican figures
whispered together as they felt the frenzy rising in many a

corral. But the premonition passed, and the wild gallop faded from Richardson's eyes as the distant Anthony wheeled into another road. He sighed and turned and went back to his rooms, while his own thoughts went out again in a perpetual aspiration beyond even the Celestials to That which created the Celestials.

In a spirit of less devotion, but shattered by—for him— wilder and less tolerable vision, the abandoned driver was leaning against his broken cart, holding it with the intensity almost of madness, and crying out perpetually—"My God! O my God!"

Chapter Eleven

THE CONVERSION OF
DAMARIS TIGHE

It was not the least among the vexations which interfered with Damaris Tighe's exposition of culture that building had begun at the back of her house. For years, indeed ever since they had come to live at Smetham, their garden had looked out over a lane and fields beyond. But quite recently the fields had been bought as a desirable building estate, and a number of villas were to be put up—villas in which it seemed probable that a very different class of people would live from collators of MSS. and students of philosophy. Or so Damaris, who knew very little about people, assumed. They would play tennis, not for an amusement but for a business; they would give parties on lawns; they would talk the jargon of motor-cars and wireless and the gossip of commerce and love. And they would shut her in on every side.

Some of them would be pleasant enough, perhaps here and there one of them would almost have a mind. But even so it probably wouldn't be the kind that would be any use to her. If it were, she could very well make use of a little help in copying and arranging and so on. But probably that was too much to hope for.

It was going on for eight on that Sunday evening when Damaris shut her books and reluctantly decided that she would call her father to supper. If he would have any; he had been eating less and less for the last day or two, and had entirely declined the cold chicken they had had for lunch, contenting himself with a little fruit. Damaris had decided that he must be ill, and she proposed to tell him at supper that she would send for the doctor on Monday. More trouble, she thought; he was probably going to have influenza, and that would mean more work for the maid, and possibly more dislocation of her already dislocated hours. Perhaps she could get him to go away for a few days; if he was going to be ill he had better be ill in a seaside hotel than at home. It would be more convenient for her, and make no particular difference to him. People could be ill anywhere, and they couldn't study bygone cultures anywhere, nor accurately plot out the graph of human thought. There was to be a graph of human thought as an appendix—three graphs actually, from 500 B.C. to A.D. 1200, showing respectively the relation of official thought, cultural thought, and popular thought to the ideas of personalized and depersonalized supernatural powers. By looking at the graph it would be quite easy to see what attitude an Athenian citizen of the age of Thucydides, an Alexandrian friend of Plotinus, or a Burgundian peasant of the Middle Ages had towards this personification. All the graphs had additional little curves running out of them, marked with certain great names. Eusebius of Caesarea, who had identified Platonic ideas with the thoughts of the Christian God, had one; so had Synesius of Cyrene—only she had mislaid her note on Synesius, and couldn't at the moment remember why he was distinguished in that way; so had William of Occam, Albert, and of course Abelard. Personification was in itself evidence of a rather low cultural state; she had called it somewhere "The mind's habit of consoling itself with ideographs." As education developed so a sense of abstraction grew up, and it became more possible to believe that the North Wind was a passage of air, and not an individual, or that St. Michael was a low-class synonym for —probably for just warfare, and justice pure and simple. Which was why he weighed the souls of mankind at Chartres. It was a good graph, and she was proud of it. There would be six appendices in all, but this and the new one on the Creation would be the most important.

She settled her papers. As she did so the air was suddenly shaken by a number of heavy thuds, accompanied by a rain of minor noises. Things at a distance were falling—a great number of things. She went quickly over to the window, and saw to her great astonishment that the newly built houses opposite her were falling in. Falling right down, rather: she stood and stared. The whole row of houses was in a state of increasing collapse. Some were already almost down, and the one nearest her even as she looked began to waver. It sagged inward, a row of bricks came slipping out of the wall, and dropped bumping to the earth. The chimney pots fairly dissolved; it was as if the whole strength of the house was melting. Damaris shrugged; she had said often enough how shameful all this modern jerry-building was, and here was her statement absolutely proved. She remained looking at it in a state of mild complacency. The inefficiency was disgusting; the thing had no backbone to it—no . . . no . . . for a moment she fought a consciousness of the word "guts" and substituted "real knowledge." It was after all the reality of one's knowledge that mattered. She *knew*—a sudden terrific crash as the roof fell in distracted and for a moment deafened her. She turned back into the room. "It's fortunate", she thought idly, "that there was no one living in them."

It was five minutes to eight. She thought abruptly, as she very often did, "O I must get it." Doctor of Philosophy —how hard she had worked for it! The . . . O the smell!

In full strength it took her, so violently that she stepped backward and made an involuntary gesture outward. The horror of it nearly made her faint. It must, she thought, be something to do with these new houses; some corrupt material had been used. The smell was corruption. Something would have to be done; the Council Surveyor must be called in. Perhaps it wouldn't be so bad downstairs. Her window faced the fallen houses; the dining-room looked the other way. She would go down and see.

The Conversion of Damaris Tighe

As she moved the sunlight that was over her papers, except for the light shadow that she herself cast, was totally obscured. A heavy blackness obliterated it in an instant; the papers, the table, all that part of the room lay in gloom. The change was so immediate that even Damaris's attention was caught, and, still wrinkling her nose at the appalling smell, she glanced half round to see what dark cloud had suddenly filled the sky. And then she did come much nearer to fainting than ever before in her life.

Outside the window something was . . . was. That was the only certainty her startled senses conveyed. There was a terrific beak protruding through the open window into the room, there was the most appalling body she had ever conceived possible; there were two huge flapping wings; there were two horrible red eyes. And there was the smell. Damaris stood stock still, gasping at it, thinking desperately, "I'm dreaming." The beastly apparition remained. It seemed to be perched there, on the window-sill or the pear-tree or something. Its eyes held her; its wings moved, as if uncertainly opening; its whole repulsive body shook and stirred; its beak—not three yards distant—jerked at her, as if the thing were stabbing; then it opened. She had a vision of great teeth; incapable of thought, she stumbled backward against the table, and remained fixed. Something in her said, "It can't be"; something else said, "It is." She'd been overworking; that must be it. It was . . . it was like spots before the eyes. It wasn't; it was detestably different. It—O God, the thing was moving. It was coming . . . it wasn't . . . it was, it was coming in. She couldn't see how; whether the window broke or melted or what, but it was certainly nearer. The beak was not much more than a yard off now; the huge leathern-like wings were opening out within the room, or partly within it. She couldn't in the fœtid darkness which was spreading round her see which was room and which was horror, but she flung herself wildly back, scrambling and scrabbling somehow across her table. Her papers went flying before her, her books, her pen—everything fell from it as Damaris Tighe, unconscious of her work for the first time for years, got herself on the table, and pushed herself somehow across it. The thing stayed still watching her; only the wings furled and unfurled themselves slowly, as if there were no hurry—no hurry at all, but what it had to do. She was half on her feet again, crouching, sliding, getting sideways towards the door, feeling for the handle, praying wildly to Anthony, to her father, to Abelard and Pythagoras, to Anthony again. If only Anthony were here! She got hold of the handle; of course that beak, those eyes, that smell—O that sickening and stupendous *smell!*—were all dreams. She was asleep; in a minute she would be outside the door, then she would wake up. In a few seconds. The little eyes gleamed greed at her. She *was* outside; she banged the door.

On the landing she leaned against the banisters, and dimly considered pulling herself together. For the first time in her life she wanted somebody very badly, somebody—but Anthony for choice. Only Anthony had been driven away that morning. Her father then. Only her father was separated from her. Somebody, *somebody* to break this awful loneliness that had settled on her, this loneliness in which the memory of that horror was her only companion. O somebody . . . somebody. "I'm being silly," she thought. What was that idea of pulling herself together? And . . . and what was that other noise? She looked up.

Over the skylight above her head she saw something dragged, and knew it for an edge of those wings. There was a noise of scratching; a crack; more scratching or what sounded like scratching. The wing disappeared; came back; went again. And again she saw the beak, thrusting down through the open skylight, stabbing, questing. All bonds of habit broken, mad and fearful of madness, she screamed out and flung herself down the stars. "Father!" she cried. "Father!" and found him standing before her in the hall.

The Conversion of Damaris Tighe

He was looking at her with that utter detachment which had come on him—not so much looking as allowing her, rather reluctantly, to be visible to him. She caught his arm, staggering, and babbling nonsense. Only sometimes she paused and clung, in frightened tears, in terror, in anguish. She didn't dare look round; she looked at him; he would know, he would see, he would do something; and she herself could do nothing at all. But in some two or three minutes she ceased, for there crept into her exhausted consciousness the thought that all this was vain. He was still looking at her, from a placid detachment, and all he said was, "Yes, yes. Well, I was afraid you might get hurt," and the very words cost him an effort, so that there seemed to be great silences betwixt them. Then as if relieved of her presence his eyes went blank, his voice changed. "Ah!" he murmured, "Ah!" and sighed happily, and pushed at her as if she were hindering him, pushed her away, back into the corruption that was growing round her in the dreadful odour which renewed itself, and was attacking her with a vehemence which made it seem the very body of the creature of her terror.

As he pushed her she loosed hold. It was some stranger who went by, and up the stairs—she gave another wild scream as he did so—a half warning, only he took no notice. He went from her, lost in the contemplation which held him, going away with his memories and his knowledge thick over and around him, abandoned by and abandoning everything but the pure certainty of beauty which he had seen. She dared not go that way; she screamed once more, and took a desparate little run. But her feet didn't seem to move easily; they were sticking, sinking; she had to pull them out of the floor, or the ground, the damp marshy ground they were toiling through. She looked down; the floor was half floor and half bog, squelchy green spreading under her in patches, which widened and joined themselves, and she was being held by them as she moved. She looked up and saw the shape of the walls and ceiling, but now spectral and growing fainter against a wide open

131

space, a vast plain, stretching emptily away to where at the horizon a heavy and inflamed sky sank to meet it. The house was no more than a shadowy diagram; all the solidity had vanished, and a mere arrangement of lines showed against the wild background. She saw it, and yet did not feel it as altogether unknown: she had somewhere been acquainted with that desolate plain. Right in front of her, beyond the framework of the front door, was the gleam of water. She dragged her feet from the mire and tried to get firmer footing, while her mind sought to remember the name of the place. She had never seen it yet she knew—O very well she knew it, and the figure that was coming towards her across it from far away, a tiny figure, so distant was it, but human. As she gazed she heard another sound above, and looked up to see the earlier horror flying round in circles high over her. There she stood on the edge of a swampy pool, with the pterodactyl wheeling round in the sky, and one remote companion. She couldn't be frightened more; her dulled mind, as she stood there helplessly, returned to that approaching form, and there again she thought she recognized something familiar in its movement. It came on quickly: it was a man wrapped in a kind of large cloak, bareheaded, bald —no, not bald, but with a head shaved in a tonsure. Her remote memory woke—it was a medieval priest; he came on towards her still more quickly, and then, though his face was strange, she knew him with a quick certainty. It was—it was Peter Abelard himself, Abelard, mature, but still filled with youth because of the high intensity of his philosophical passion, and he was singing as he came: singing the words that he had himself composed, and which a voice of her own past had spoken to her but lately:

> *O quanta qualia*
> *sunt illa Sabbata.*

Against that angry sky he came on, in that empty land his voice rang out in joy, and she tried to move; she ran a few steps forward, and made an effort to speak. Her voice failed; she heard herself making grotesque noises in her throat, and suddenly over him there fell the ominous shadow of the pterodactyl. Only for a few seconds, then it passed on, and he emerged from it, and his face was towards her, but now it had changed. Now it was like a vile corpse, and yet still it was uttering things: it croaked at her in answer to her own croakings, strange and meaningless words. *Individualiter, essentialiter, categoricorum, differentia substantialis*—croak, croak, croak. He was coming towards her, and she was trying to run away; and now the blackness had fallen on them both, and the horrid presence of that other filthy being had swept down. She shrieked and stumbled and fell and it caught her.

Something touched her face: something swept her arm; something enveloped and weighed against her heart. Her eyes were shut; she had no power to look again. Her brain was dazed; she had no power to think. Her mouth was panting horribly; and from it, wrenched by a physical power from a physical consciousness, there came one last and feeble and continuous effort to call Anthony."An . . . An . . . A . . . A . . . A . . ." she was saying, and the effort became mere gasps as she shook and shrank. There was something which could save her —something if that something would come. She lay in a heap and the great flap of great wings beat over her, and she felt them pressing her, and something had hurt her head. "A . . . A . . . A . . ." she went on moaning, and claws pressed the back of her neck, dreadful, horrible claws. The smell was working within her; in some way it was Abelard. It was Abelard, and the wings lifted and again caught her. She was on her face on the marshy ground, and she was being forced over. As well as she could she hid herself, but it was all in vain. There was nothing round her but a hideous and vile corruption, nothing, nothing except a vibration that went rhythmically through her, as if—almost from somewhere within her—a horse were galloping. And then she heard her name.

The Conversion of Damaris Tighe

It wasn't cried aloud; it was spoken as normally as it had been spoken a hundred times in that place—the state of knowledge. When she heard it she felt herself straining to hear it again, and did, but this time with a note of command in it, so that in a hasty obedience she opened her eyes. That was what, by nothing but her name speeded on music, she had been bidden to do. She obeyed; not easily, but she obeyed.

Anthony was standing near her, and behind him was the brightness of a sky lovely in a summer sunset. His arm was stretched out towards her, and she felt the weight upon her lifting. He called to her by her name, and she answered with his own, with the name of which she had cried for help, but hardly murmured now, so spent was she. Nevertheless as she breathed it she felt herself free, and then there was the shade of wings in the air, and another flying thing sailed into sight and floated slowly down to his shoulder. There, eagle-plumaged, eagle-beaked, eagle eyed, it rested; he raised his hand, and as if in an august leniency it allowed itself to be caressed. His eyes, as he leaned his head aside, full of love and loving laughter, rested on hers. She received with joy both love and laughter; there went out from him, and from the Augustitude upon his shoulder, a knowledge of safety would she but take it, and freely and humbly she let it enter her being. The thing she had rejected and yet used gathered and expanded round him as if a glory attended him. He looked down at her, and though she longed for him to gather her and let her feel more closely the high protection of his power, she was content to wait upon his will. As she made that motion of assent she felt the wildness of the desolate plain shut out. A covering formed over them and hid the sky; shelter was restored, and when at last he moved and came to her, and she half-raised herself to meet him, her hand touched the mat at the dining-room door, and she knew she was lying again in her own house. As he moved the eagle-form left his shoulder, swept up and round, passed her and disappeared in the shadows of the room.

The Conversion of Damaris Tighe

But she had not time for that fantastic dream; she looked at her cousin, and felt that either she or he had changed. There was in him something which shook her with a fear, but with a fear very different from that which she had felt but now. This was power and intelligence; this was command. He came over to her, stretching out his hands, and said as he took hers: "You were only just in time, weren't you, dearest?"

"Yes," she said, and got to her feet, holding tightly to his grasp. He put his arm round her, and took her to a chair, and stood for awhile in front of her silent. She said suddenly: "What was it?"

He looked at her gravely. "I wonder what you'll say if I tell you," he said.

"I shall believe you," she answered simply. "Anthony, I'm . . . I'm sorry."

The laughter broke out again in his eyes. "And why are you sorry, my cousin?" he asked.

"I've behaved very badly," Damaris said. To tell him seemed to her more important than anything else in the world could be, even the vanished monstrosity.

Anthony took her hand again, and kissed it. "And *how* have you behaved badly, my cousin?" he asked.

"I've tried to make use of you," Damaris said, beginning to blush. "I've been . . . I've been . . ."

". . . the first-born of Lilith, who is illusion, and Samael the Accursed," Anthony finished. "Yes, darling. But that doesn't matter between us. It isn't that which you saw."

"What was it?" Damaris asked shuddering and looking round in a renewed servile fear. Even as she did so he released his hand from hers and stepped back, so that, as she moved hastily to catch hold of him again, he was beyond her reach, and as he spoke there was a sternness in his voice.

"You saw what you know," he said, "and because it's the only thing you know you saw like that. You've been told about it often enough; you've been warned and warned again. You've

135

had it whispered to you and shouted at you—but you wouldn't stop or think or believe. And what you wouldn't hear about you've seen, and if you're still capable of thanking God you'd better do it now. You, with your chatter about this and the other, your plottings and plannings, and your little diagrams, and your neat tables—what did you think you would make of the agonies and joys of the masters? O I know such things must be: we must shape to ourselves the patterns in what they said—man must use his mind. But you've done more than use it, you've loved it for your own. You've loved it and you've lost it. And pray God you've lost it before it was too late, before it decayed in you and sent up that stink which you smelt, or before the knowledge of life turned to the knowledge of death. Somewhere in you there was something that loved truth, and if ever you studied anything you'd better study that now. For perhaps you won't get another chance."

She put out her hand for his. "But tell me," she said, "I don't understand. What ought I to do? How can that thing . . . that horrible thing . . . what do you mean? Anthony, tell me. I know I've tried to use you. . . ."

"You've tried to use something else than me," Anthony said more gently, but he did not take her hand. "And it's up to you to stop. Or not."

"I'll try to stop if you think I ought to," Damaris said. "But what did I see?"

"I'll tell you," he said, "if you want me to. Do you want me to?"

She gripped him suddenly. "Why did you come to me?" she exclaimed, and he answered simply, "Because I heard you call."

"Tell me," she said, and he begun, going over the tale as it had been known to him. But he spoke now neither with the irritation nor with the amusement which she had felt in him of old; his voice convinced her of what he said, and the authority that was in it directed and encouraged even while it awed and warned her. He neither doubted nor permitted her to doubt; the whole gospel—morals and mythology at once—entered into and possessed her. When he came to speak of Quentin's flight she trembled a little as she sat and tried to move her hand away. But Anthony, standing above her and looking out towards the darkening eastern sky, did not release it; half a chain and half a caress, his own retained hers by the same compulsion that she heard in his voice, and he exposed her to the knowledge of what she had done. Merciless and merciful, he held her; pitiful and unpitying, he subordinated her to the complete realization of herself and her past.

"So", he ended at last, "we can't tell what will happen. But I don't think", he added, his voice lightening, "that there is much time left before it does. I shall know presently what I have to do."

After a long silence she said, "Do you know, Anthony, I think perhaps I ought. . . ." She paused.

"Ought?" he asked.

"Ought to go and look for your friend."

He considered it gravely. "I had expected to do it myself," he said, "but I don't feel that I ought. . . . There's some other thing . . . Why will you go?"

"It's either that or Abelard," she said, smiling faintly. "My father doesn't want me."

"No," he answered. "I think your father's almost dead already. I thought so when he let me in just now—before I found you lying on the floor."

She shuddered again. "O darling, it was dreadful when he pushed me away," she said, and he answered again, looking down on her, tender and stern at once: "And you—if it comes to pushing away?"

In such conversation, question and answer exchanged between them while Damaris searched her heart, and the dark places where the images of obscene profanations dwelt, they stayed for a long time. They did not hear the noise where, at the back of the house, a crowd surged and pushed and stared and laughed and talked round the fallen houses, and told one another how here a boarding and there a fence had also given way, and how funny it was. Nor did they interrupt above them the trance that was increasing upon her father where he lay stretched on his bed, content now not even to move, and aware only of the vision of living colour that possessed him, as the beauty to which he had offered himself accepted inevitably that surrender, and softly gathered him into itself. In the town the living outposts of the invasion awaited it—Richardson and Foster and Dora Wilmot—each after their kind. Beyond the town change was proceeding; in a great circle round that solitary house there was no living thing but a few men and women, unconscious yet of the doom. Birds and insects and animals had all vanished—all but the sheep; they alone in their field seemed to know nothing of the Angels of that other world. And even among these Principles and Dominations perhaps none but that Virtue which Anthony had encountered in the pit, and which in its earthly image had deigned to be with him that night when he came to dissipate the fear of that other image which was yet itself to the challenge of the presumptuous and erring mind—none but the Virtue understood, in its soaring comprehension, the safety in which the sheep still lived, or from what yet deeper distance of spirit was to arise the Innocence which everlastingly formed and maintained them.

Chapter Twelve

THE TRIUMPH OF THE ANGELICALS

Richardson, returning towards his rooms, decided suddenly not to enter them.

The sweep and wonder of his vision were still with him; his body still palpitated with the echo of those charging hooves, though within him his spirit desired a further end. He longed to approach that other end with the speed of the racing herd, but to such an approach the intoxication of the sight was alien; he subdued himself harshly. Visions and auditions had nothing to do with the final surrender, which was—for him—a thing to be achieved wholly in itself, and (it seemed) without reference to any natural or supernatural event. A lonely life had but emphasized, as the exterior life will, the interior method which he pursued. Even his connexion with Berringer had been but a part of a distraction necessary and right to relieve the rigour of his duty, and to keep him in spiritual health, but not part of that duty. Chance, assisted by his personal tastes, had given him a job among books, and as far as possible he read in those books of the many ways which are always the Way. But not by books or by phrases, not by images or symbols or myths, did he himself follow it. He abstracted himself continually from sense and from thought, attempting always a return to an interior nothingness where that which is itself no thing might communicate its sole essential being.

So separating himself from the memory of the horses, so concentrated on the Nothing of his desires, he walked for some time along the streets until he experienced the easily recognized symptoms of temporary interior exhaustion. Obedient to those symptoms he relaxed and murmured to himself, as was his habit at such conclusions, the phrases from the Dionysius with whom Damaris had been concerned—"He hath not power, nor is he power; He liveth not, nor is He life; neither is He of the things that are or are not, nor is there for Him any word of name or thought, for He is neither darkness nor light, neither error nor truth." As he ended he began again to look round him. He was standing half-way down a street in one of the rather poorer parts of the town—where the lower middle-class were slightly more obviously lower. A tobacconist close by was shutting up for the night; the two recognized each other and nodded.

"Funny business about the telephones," the tobacconist said.

"I hadn't heard," Richardson answered casually but politely. "What was it?"

The tobacconist paused in his task. "All down, so they say," he explained. "I had occasion to want to speak to my brother in London—my wife thought she'd run up to-morrow by the cheap train—and the Exchange girl told me I couldn't get through! Couldn't get a trunk call through on Sunday night! All nonsense it sounded to me, and so I told her, and she as good as told me not to be a fool—the lines were down. They've sent out repair gangs, it seems; I had old Mr. Hoskins in—you know him, I expect; the grandfather, I mean; comes in for his quarter-pound every Sunday evening as regularly as the sun . . . well, I ought to say moon, oughtn't I? at this time of day, but one gets into a habit of speaking."

"One does," Richardson murmured in the pause. "Unless one is careful."

"So he told me", the tobacconist resumed, "that the poles have fallen down—all along the roads—all smashed to bits they are, he said, and the wires all fused and broken. Most extraordinary thing I ever heard of. Old Hoskins, he thought it must have been the wind, but then as I said to him: 'Where's the wind?' Now my belief is that it's got something to do with all that thunder we've been having the last few days—this electricity's a funny thing. Don't you think that's more likely now, sir?"

Richardson nodded; then seeing that he was expected to speak, said, "It's certain, I should think, to have something to do with the thunder."

"And as for hoardings and fences I hear they're down in a lot of places. Funny thing altogether."

"Very funny," Richardson answered. "Awkward if the houses follow suit."

The tobacconist gaped at him for a moment. "O I don't think that's likely," he began slowly, but looking up at his own first floor with the beginnings of a fearful anxiety. "I mean houses are rather different to hoardings, aren't they?"

"Houses that have been lived in, perhaps," Richardson acknowledged, also looking thoughtfully upwards. "Yes, perhaps. There may be an infiltration of human existence . . ." He ceased and seemed to await a decision.

"Yes," the tobacconist said, recovering faith. "Human beings make all the difference, don't they? A little bit of furniture works wonders in an empty house. Why, when we moved in here, I said to my wife about a room where there was nothing had been put but a chair that had got a leg broken— my fault it was—in the shifting—not a carpet down there wasn't nothing but that bit of chair, and I said to her: 'It looks like home already.' Just the difference between a room and four walls and a floor."

"Is there any?" Richardson asked. "Yes, of course, I see what you mean." But his spirit cried out that there was in fact no difference; they were alike shape and form and so far temptations to the soul which so long sought refuge in such exterior patterns from the state in which no such patterns were to be found or desired. He felt the contrast so sharply that he could endure no more talk; he forced himself to say, with as little abruptness as possible, "Ah, well, I daresay we shall hear more

141

about it in the morning," nodded a goodnight and crossed the road.

As he reached the other side he saw before him a church. It was a small, old, rather ugly Wesleyan church; the doors were open because of the heat, and apparently the service was not yet over. Richardson, casually attracted, looked at his watch: nearly nine. He paused on the pavement and looked in. It must, he thought, be some kind of after-service, and, after a few moments' search, the notice-board confirmed the idea. On the third Sunday in the month there was apparently the Breaking of Bread. It must, he thought, be a rather out-of-date place; most of the Nonconforming Churches had adopted the words "Holy Communion." Besides, this building still called itself "Zion," which was surely a rather old-fashioned title. But perhaps he was wrong; he didn't pretend to be an expert in ecclesiology. All that sort of thing was very well for the minds that could use it; he couldn't use it, neither the small dull gatherings of the Evangelicals or the large gaudy assemblies of the Catholics. "The flight of the alone to the Alone." But no doubt this was proper to them—if it increased their speed upon the Way. Speed, speed, and always speed! His mind remembered that wild careering herd; so, and swifter than so, he desired the Return. He seemed to hear the beating hooves again, and while for a moment he attended to that interior echo something huge and rapid drove past him and into the church. Certainly he had felt it, though there was nothing visible, but he had felt the movement of a body and heard the sound of hooves. Within him his chief concern renewed itself in a burst of imperious ardour; he burned towards the—no, not fire; no, not darkness; no words, no thought, nothing but . . . nothing but . . . well, *but*—that which was when all other "buts" had been removed, and all hindrances abolished. For a moment he felt a premonition; something wholly new and exquisite touched him and was gone.

He was standing in front of the church and looking into it.

The Triumph of the Angelicals

There didn't seem to be many there; one or two figures were moving at the upper end; a few more were scattered about the small building. They were seated as if waiting—perhaps for the Breaking of Bread; and as he gazed a gleam of extreme brightness struck through the building and vanished, for the lights within had flashed upon something moving that caught and reflected their radiance in one shining curve as if a sword had been swung right across the church. Blinded by its intensity he took a step back, then he recovered and looked again. This time—and his spirit livened again with his habitual desire—he saw it. It was standing at the other end of Zion; it was something like a horse in shape and size, but of a dazzling whiteness, and from the middle of its forehead there grew a single horn. He recognized the myth of poems and pictures; he saw the Divine Unicorn gently sustaining itself in that obscure and remote settlement of the faithful. He recognized the myth, but he recognized something else too, only he could not put a name to it. The thing moved, pure and stately, a few paces down the aisle, and as it did so he was transported within himself a million miles upon his way. It moved with the beauty of swiftness, however small the distance was that it went; it lowered and tossed its head, and again that gleaming horn caught all the light in Zion, and gathered it, and flashed it back in a dazzling curve of purity. As the brightness passed he saw that within they were still intent upon the service; the deacons were bearing the Bread of the Communion to the few who were there, and as they did so it seemed to the watcher that the unicorn moved its head gently in the direction of each, nay, that some eidolon of itself, though it remained unchanged in the centre, went very swiftly to each, and then he lost sight of the images. Only now he was aware—and only aware—of a sensation of rushing speed passing through his being; it was not for him to adore the unicorn; he was the unicorn. He and those within, and others—who and when and where he did not know, but others—a great multitude whom no man could number—they went swiftly, they were hastening to an end. And again the shining horn flung back the earthly lights around it, and in that reflection the seeker knew himself speeding to his doom. So slow, so slow, the Way had seemed; so swiftly, so swiftly, through aeons and universes, the Principle, the Angel of man's concern, went onwards in unfailing strength. Yet it had not moved; it stood there still, showing itself, as if in a moment's dream, to the fellows of devotion, so that each beheld and supposing it to be a second's fantasy determined not to speak of it. But pure and high the ardour burned in every soul, as Zion shone in Zion, and time hastened to its conclusion in them. The minister gave out a hymn; the voices began it; the great beast of revelation that stood there moved again, and as Richardson unconsciously moved also he felt his arm caught from behind.

Startled and constraining himself, he turned his head. Behind him, a little to his left, clutching his arm, and staring at him with fierce bloodshot eyes, stood Foster. For a few seconds Richardson did not take in the fact; the two remained staring. Then, he could not have told why, he broke into a little laugh; Foster snarled at him, and the hand that was on the other's arm seemed to clutch and drag at it. Richardson took a step or two backward, his eyes going once more to the aisle as he did so. But this time he could see nothing unusual; indeed, he felt doubtful already of what he had seen, only he knew that there was working within him a swiftness more than he had ever dreamed. The hesitations and sloths that had often hampered him had vanished; he looked at Foster from a distance, down a precipice from the forest of the unicorn to the plain of the lion.

Foster said, "It's here."

"It's always here," the younger man answered, "but we have to go a long way to find it."

"Have you got the strength?" Foster asked. He was speaking thickly and with difficulty; the voice blurred itself in the middle of the sentence, and the last word came out almost booming. His face was red, and his shoulders heaving; when he ceased to speak Richardson noticed that his breath was coming in great pants, as if he were struggling against some oppression at his heart. The sight brought back the other's attention; he looked at Foster and gently disengaged himself, saying quietly, "What's the strength to you or me? was that what we went in to it for? Speed now, and at that only the right speed."

"Speed enough too," Foster answered deeply. "Speed to hunt, strength to kill. Are you for them or are you like that other jackanapes that thought he could stand in the way—in the way of the lion?" The voice rose into a roar and he scrabbled with his feet on the pavement.

Richardson, now completely watchful, said, "It seems that you're with them entirely now."

"I'm looking for him," Foster said, "for him, and"—he began to snarl, "and—and others. There's—ah! ah!—there's a man in my off—off—office," he barely achieved the word, "that I hate, I hate his face, I'll look after him. The strength'll be on him. Look, look for him, I'll look."

He turned his eyes about him; his mouth opened and his lips curled back over his teeth. Then he seemed to make an effort towards control, and began to mutter something to himself. "Not much yet, lord god!" Richardson heard. "Slowly, lord, slowly! I'll make sacrifice—the blood of the sacrifice," and at that a sudden impatient anger caught the young man.

"Fool," he cried out, "there's only one sacrifice, and the God of gods makes it, not you."

Foster did not seem to hear, and Richardson almost at once regretted the outburst. Something in it offended him; it was a pit laid for the silver hooves of an immaculate and solitary virtue that was galloping away, away in the cool light of the stars, amid rivers of chastity, to gardens high up among the snows. There—there—it would find its lair and sleep alone among the trees of Eden before man had fallen and . . .

Images, images, he caught his mind back, abolishing them; beyond images, byond any created shape or invented fable lay the union of the end. He was lost in his intensity and woke to awareness again to hear Foster saying,

". . . the chosen. The chosen are few. Even the woman . . . if I knew . . . knew. The gods know; the gods are here. Here!"

The word went up in a roar up the street. Richardson heard a startled exclamation behind him. He looked round—the worshippers were coming out of Zion, and one of them, an old gentleman with his wife, had jumped violently at the noise. A dismayed voice exclaimed, "Really, really!" A more indignant feminine voice said, "Disgusting! It's enough to deafen anyone."

But the bleating of an innocent mortality had no effect on the possessed being before them. He glared round him, then he threw up his head, and began to sniff softly and horribly, as if he were seeking to find a trail. The old gentleman stared, then he said to Richardson, in a voice not quite steady, "Ill, is he?"

"O if he's ill," the old lady said in a tone of pity. "Would he like to come in and sit down for a few minutes? We live close by."

"Yes, do," the old gentleman added. "A little rest—when my wife comes over faint—— Well, Martha dear, you *do* sometimes come over faint."

"There's ways of being bad besides coming over faint," the old lady, now rather pink, but still sweetly anxious to help, said, "Do come in."

"Thank you very much indeed," Richardson said gravely, "but I'm afraid it wouldn't help." And then, by an irresistible impulse, "I hope you had a happy service?"

They both looked at him with delight. "Now that's very kind," the old gentleman said. "Thank you, sir, it was a very beautiful service."

146

"Beautiful," the old lady said. She hesitated, fumbling with her umbrella; then, taking sudden courage, she took a step towards Richardson and went on, "You'll excuse me, sir, I know it's old-fashioned, and you quite a stranger, but—are you saved?"

Richardson answered her as seriously as she had spoken, "I believe salvation is for all who will have it," he said,"and I will have it by the only possible means."

"Ah, that's good, that's good," the old gentleman said. "Bless God for it, young man."

"I know you'll pardon me, sir," the old lady added, "you being a stranger as I said, and strangers often not liking to talk about it. Though what else there is to talk about . . ."

"What indeed?" Richardson agreed, and again through the evening there struck upon his ears the noise of galloping hooves, and for a moment the whole earth upon which he stood seemed to be a charging beast upon which he rode, faster than ever his own haste could carry him. But the sound, if it were a sound, struck at the same time on that other creature, half-transfigured, who stood in front of him still. It sprang up, it bellowed out some half-formed word, then it broke off and went leaping down the street; and amazed or meditative the three watched it go.

"Dear me," the old lady said; and the old gentleman, "He's behaving very strangely, isn't he?"

Richardson nodded. "Very strangely. I'm afraid, but—" he sought a phrase at once mutually comprehensible, comforting, and true—"but he's in the hands of God."

"Still——" the old gentleman said dubiously. But there was nothing to be done, so they parted and went their way, leaving Richardson standing by the now closed church. The other members of the congregation had come out during the brief conversation and gone. He considered vaguely what to do. And then he remembered Dora Wilmot.

He had spoken of her to Anthony the day before as one of

those who desired the power of the Immortals, the virtue of the things that they sought, not for that virtue's sake, not even for the sake of fresh and greater experiences, but merely that their old experience might be more satisfactory to them. Foster wanted to be stronger than those with whom he came in contact; he had made himself a place for the lion and it seemed the lion was taking possession of its habitation; its roar echoing in the wilderness and the dry places of the soul. Dora Wilmot had never dreamed of such brutal government; but once Richardson had caught the expression in her eyes as she handed a cup of coffee to Mrs. Rockbotham, and any quiet little supper with the—probably slandered—children of the Lord Alexander VI would have seemed to him preferable. And if there had entered into her some subtlety from that world, what was happening to her? or, perhaps more important, what was she doing? It occurred to him that he might go and see; almost at the same time it occurred to him, as he still watched the old lady stepping down the street beside her husband, that he might perhaps—not stop her but offer her an alternative course, if it seemed possible or desirable. After all, that old lady had wanted to be kind, even if she reduced indescribable complexities of experience to an epigram. His own solitary life had rather left him without any formed habit of being kind, he reflected: perhaps he was a little too much inclined to concentrate on an end which was (all the authorities assured him) largely dependent on the way. Anthony Durrant had gone charging off to some unknown Damaris. Berringer had been kind to him. Very well, he would go and see if the road of the unicorn led through the house of Dora Wilmot.

When he arrived there he was, after inquiry, shown in to the room where Anthony had fought with the beasts. Miss Wilmot, thin and sedate, was at her writing table. Several little sealed envelopes lay in a pile at one side: she put down her pen as he entered. They looked at one another with doubt masked by courtesy, and exchanged a few trifling remarks. Then Richardson said, "And what do you make of it all, Miss Wilmot?"

She answered softly. "Have you seen Mr. Foster?"

"Yes," Richardson admitted. "But only just now. That must be my excuse for calling so late." On the Day of Judgment, if there were another, one would probably say things like that, he thought. But he went on swiftly. "And, to tell you the truth, I don't much like Mr. Foster at the moment."

"I shouldn't expect you to," she said. "For you . . . he . . . we aren't meaning . . ." She was almost stammering, as if she were trying to say several things at once, but under his eyes she made an effort to be collected. Her eyes, nevertheless, went on shooting from side to side, and her restless arms twisted themselves together and again untwisted as she sat.

"You aren't meaning——?"

"We wouldn't . . . we shouldn't . . . find it likely . . . that you . . ." Suddenly she gave a little tortured scream. "O!" she cried, "O! I can't keep up! it keeps dividing! There's too many things to think of!"

He got up and went nearer to her, very watchful. But with an unusual note of pity in his voice he said, "Need you think of them?"

"O yes . . ." she breathed, "yes-s. There's the wretch-ch of a Rockbotham. I've done hers-s, and Mrs Jacquelin, I've done hers. Such a nice, ni-c-ce one, and I'm s-scribbing this-s to the one that s-spoke, the Damaris creature—but sh-she's strange, so-s I had to s-ese what was bes-st."

She looked up at him malevolently as he stood over her, and with the end of her tongue moistened her lips. Then her eyes changed again and terror came into them, and in a voice from which the dreadful sibilance had departed she cried out, "My head, my head! There's too much to see, there's so many ways of doing it! I can't think."

Richardson laid his hand on hers. "There is one thing very

149

certain," he said with firm clearness, "the way to the Maker of the Gods."

She looked sly. "Will he help me to show old Mother Rock-botham what her husband might be like?" she said. "Or old Jackie what that nephew of hers is doing?" Her eyes went to the sealed letters. "They didn't think much of me," she said. "I could sit here and do their work. But I'm getting my turn now. If only I could see them reading their letters."

Richardson gathered both her hands, as they lay on the writing table into one of his, and almost released them again as he did so. They were clammy-cold and they wriggled horribly in his grasp. But he held them while he leant quickly across and caught up the little pile of letters; then he released them and sprang back. "What devilry have you been up to?" he asked her harshly. "What are these letters you're so proud of?"

"I was afraid at first," she said, "but he told me—Foster told me—they would help us, strength and subtlety, he said. And . . . and . . . O my head! my head!"

She tried to stand up and could not; she writhed in her chair; but her eyes were fixed on him, and their immediate pain changed as his met them into malice and fear. He ripped a letter open and glanced at it, and as he did so she slithered down and began to wriggle towards him across the floor. He had time only for the first few sentences, and a hasty glance at the middle and the end, but they told him all he needed to know. The letter was to Mrs. Rockbotham; it opened with sympathetic phrases of sorrow, then it went on, with a careful and subtle art he had not time then to admire, to bite with stored venom at the heart. The doctor was . . . he was . . . for the moment Richardson did not grasp what he was; some evil was suggested, or something that would seem evil to the reader—perversion and cruelty, was it? "Take care of yourself," one sentence began, and the thing wasn't signed—yes, it was: "From a Sister in Trouble." He crumpled it in his hand and leapt aside as a hand touched his ankle, then he ran for the door and shouted for the maid. When she showed herself, "Telephone for the doctor," he called, "your mistress is ill." Then thrusting the letters in his pocket he went back into the room.

She was where he had left her, but a dreadful change was coming over her. Her body was writhing into curves and knots where she lay, as if cramps convulsed her. Her mouth was open, but she could not scream: her hands were clutching at her twisted throat. In her wide eyes there was now no malice, only an agony, and gradually all her body and head were drawn up backwards from the floor by an invisible force, so that from the hips she remained rigidly upright and her legs lay stretched straight out behind her upon the ground, as if a serpent in human shape raised itself before him. The sight drove him backwards; he turned his face away, and prayed with all his strength to the Maker of the Celestials. From that refuge he looked again, and saw her convulsed and convulsed with spasms of anguish. But now the very colour of her skin was changing; it became blotched and blurred with black and yellow and green; not only that but it seemed distended about her. The face rounded out till it was perfectly smooth, with no hollows or depressions, and from her nostrils and her mouth something was thrusting out. In and out of her neck and hands another skin was forming, over or under her own—he could not distinguish which, but growing through it, here a coating, there an underveiling. Another and an inhuman tongue was flickering out over a human face, and the legs were twisted and thrown from side to side as if something prisoned in them were attempting to escape. For all that lower violence her body did not fall, nor indeed, but for a slight swaying, did it much move. Her arms were interlocked in front of her, the extreme ends of her fingers touched the ground between her thighs. But they too were drawn inwards; the stuff of her dress was rending in places; and wherever it rent and hung aside he could see that other curiously-toned skin shining behind it. A black shadow was on her face; a huge shape was emerging from it, from her, growing larger and larger as the Domination she had invoked freed itself from the will and the mind and the body that had given it a place where it could find the earth for its immaterialization. No longer a woman but a serpent indeed surged before him in the darkening room, bursting and breaking from the woman's shape behind it. It curved and twined itself in the last achievements of liberty; there came through the silence that had accompanied that transmutation a sound as if some slight thing had dropped to the floor, and the Angelic energy was wholly free.

It was free. It glided a little forward, and its head turned lowly from side to side. Richardson stood up and faced it. The subtle eyes gazed at him, without hostility, without friendship, remote and alien. He looked back, wordlessly calling on the Maker and End of all created energies. Images poured through his brain in an unceasing riot; questions such as Anthony had recounted to him propounded themselves; there seemed to be a million things he might do, and he did none of them. He remembered the Will beyond all the makings; then with a tremendous effort he shut out even that troublesome idea of the Will—an invented word, a mortal thought—and, as far as he could, was not before what was. It had mercy on him; he saw the great snake begin to move again, and then he fainted right away.

When he came to himself he found Dr. Rockbotham in the room, and other people, people who were carrying something out. The doctor, as soon as he discovered that the young man was conscious, came over to him, and was at first discreetly cheerful. But in a few minutes he allowed himself to relax, and said very seriously, "What happened?"

"God knows," Richardson said, and paused. Then he added, "What was she like?"

Dr. Rockbotham shook his head and—even he—shuddered.

"Dreadful," he said. "I suppose there'll have to be a post-mortem—and I hate the idea. I never want to see it again."

"God help her," Richardson said sincerely, "wherever, after death, she is. It was a dreadful chance that brought her to it. There are enough of her kind about, but the others get off scot-free."

But his thoughts were elsewhere. He looked round the room; there was no sign of the Power he had seen. The window was wide open at the bottom, and the garden lay beyond —perhaps it had passed upon its way. The end of everything was surely very near. He got to his feet.

"But you must tell me something," the doctor said. "I was wondering if I ought to call in the police."

Richardson looked at him, and mentally refused to speak. The Gods who had come to man he felt he might have to meet, but he simply couldn't explain. He uttered a few words explaining that he had been seized with faintness—which the doctor already knew—and felt he must get home. Somehow he escaped. In the street he remembered the old lady. "Certainly", he said to himself grimly, "there *are* other ways of feeling bad besides coming over faint."

Chapter Thirteen

THE BURNING HOUSE

Smetham next morning found itself more than a little agitated. It was, to begin with, on one side cut off from the outer world; the telephones and telegraphs were down. Even the railway line had been interfered with; fortunately on that side it was a very small railway, a mere branch line. But still, at a certain point the lines had simply disappeared, had apparently just crumbled into dust. The point happened to be about five yards long when it was first discovered, and by the time the railway gang got to it, it was rather more than six. There was a good deal of difficulty too about mending it—though the news of this did not reach the town till later; none of the usual appliances were reliable; they seemed to have none of their proper strength. Steel bent; wood snapped; hammers went awry, for their weight lightened even between the upward swing and the blow. It was all most unusual and very disconcerting; and those whose business or pleasure took them to the station where they found that the little train remained the whole day were thoroughly upset.

But there were others who were disturbed too. The collapse of the houses behind the Tighes' home was only part of a disturbance that affected a complete arc of the town. In that arc all dissociated buildings had been affected—by wind, by thunder, by a local earthquake, nobody knew how; sheds and garages were found to be broken down and ruinous. Hoardings were down, poles and posts—everything that was not largely used by man and that had not received into it, as matter will, over a long period, part of his more intimate life. The destruction therefore, consistent with its own laws, was inconsistent to uninstructed eyes. A shed where two small boys found continual pleasure in playing and working was left standing; a very much finer summer-house which no-one had wanted or used was found so broken up that it was not much more that a heap of splinters. Strength, though no-one realized it, was being withdrawn from the works of man, for the earth was more and more passing into the circle round the solitary house, and as it passed the Principle of Strength re-assumed all of itself which had been used in human labours. Anthony Durrant, at breakfast in the Station Hotel, heard of this and that piece of destruction, and saw it in the light of that greater knowledge which he had received since, in the abyss, he had accepted the challenge of the Eagle. This was the first circle, the extreme outward change which the entrance of man's world into that other world was producing. Over the coffee and his first cigarette he asked himself what other change was imminent. When everything was drawn farther, into the second circle—silly words, but they had to be used—when Subtlety which was the Serpent began to draw into itself the subtleties of man? A tremor went through him, but he sat on, constraining himself gravely to contemplate the possible result. For the principle of subtlety was double—instinctive and intel-lectual, and if man's intellect began to fail, or at least all unpre-pared and undefended intellect, what dreadful fatuity would take its place! He had a vision of the town full of a crowd of expressionless gaping mindless creatures, physical and mental energy passing out of them. Yet since man was meant to be the balance and pattern of all the Ideas—ah, but he was *meant* to be! Was he? Setting aside any who had deliberately aban-doned themselves to their own desires instead of the passion for truth, for reality, such as those with whom he had fought, still there were those who had unconsciously become lost in one pursuit, such as Mr. Tighe, or who had studied reality for their own purposes—such as Damaris had been. She had been saved by a terrible experience, and by the chance of (he found

himself bound to admit it as an unimportant fact) his own
devotion to her. But of the others?

He left the problem. He had his own business to attend to.
Damaris, whatever her faults, had never been a fool—outside
one particular folly—and in the long talk that they had had
on the previous evening she had grown more and more clear
that her business was to go out into the lanes and fields and see
if she could find Quentin. His breath came a little quicker;
his body shook for a moment, as he considered her making this
adventure in a countryside where such Powers were to be experienced. But he overcame this natural fear. If Damaris felt
it to be her duty, a necessity of her new life, she had better go.
In every way it would be wiser and greater than for her to
crouch over her books again while transmutation was proceeding. These cries of the soul produced their own capacities,
and though too often the capacity faded as the crisis passed, it
was better to make use of it at once than to find reasons for
neglecting it. He had himself half-intended to search for his
friend—at first alone, and then in company with Damaris, but
another place, though not another quest, had presented itself
to him. As he thought of Quentin he found his mind recurring
continually to the rooms they shared, to the long discussions,
the immortal evenings, experienced reality, eternal knowledge.
Even from the ordinary point of view, it was at least possible
that the distracted Quentin might have tried to get back to the
place he knew so well, perhaps by train if his habits still had
power on him, perhaps on foot if they had not. It was at least
as likely that Quentin would be there as anywhere, taking
refuge amid dear familiarities from his intolerable fear. But
Anthony felt that this possibility was not the real reason of his
own decision. He felt that there rather than elsewhere could
he best serve his friend; his nature go out to him, and his will be
ready. For there, in so far as place mattered at all, was the
place of the Principle that had held them together—something
that, he hoped, was stronger than the lion and subtler than the

serpent and more lovely than butterflies, something perhaps
that held even the Ideas in their places and made a tender
mockery even of the Angelicals. There his being would have
the best possibility of knowing where that other being was;
and in his new-found union with Damaris the possibility was
increased. It was for her to prove her own courage and
purpose—he could not help her there; except by accepting it.
But if her search went among—not the fields alone but those
things which moved in the fields, and if he attended, under the
protection of the Eagle, in—not their rooms alone but the place
that held their rooms, might not some success be granted, and
Quentin be brought safely from the chaos that had fallen on
him? And even . . . But the further thought eluded him;
some greater possibility flickered in his mind and was gone.
Well, that could wait; there was order even in the Divine
Hierarchies, and his first business was to catch the earliest
possible train to London.

He failed in this because Richardson telephoned just as he
was getting up from the breakfast table, and afterwards came
immediately round to see him. The tales they each had to
recount made no alteration in either of their purposes. Anthony was still clear he had to go to London, and Richardson—smiling a little ironically—proposed to go as usual to his
bookshop. They were both in very different ways too far
practised in self-discipline and intellectual control not to be
content in any crisis, even the most fantastic, to deal as
adequately as possible with the next moment. The next
moment clearly invited each of them to a definite job, and each
of them immediately responded. They shook hands and parted
at the door of the hotel, two young men separating pleasantly
for the week's work, two princely seekers after holiness dividing
to their lonely individual labours. But as they shook hands they
were, each of them, intensely aware of sound and movement
in the air about them, though one seemed rather to welcome
and one to refuse it; and those who passed either of them in the

street threw more than one glance at the intent and noble figure that went vigilantly on its way.

Among those who passed Richardson was Mr. Berringer's housekeeper. She had spent the Sunday night in Smetham, rather against the will of the male nurse whom Dr. Rockbotham had engaged. But the doctor himself had given her permission when he had been at *The Joinings* on the Sunday morning, after asking Lorrigan, which was the nurse's name, whether that wouldn't be all right. The question so obviously was one of those which the Latin grammar states are introduced by the word "nonne" that the doctor had hardly waited for the affirmative answer which "nonne" expects. What, as a matter of fact, Lorrigan had said sounded itself more like "nonne" than any English word had a right to do. He rather disapproved of having to get his own breakfast, but later on the sight of the supper which the housekeeper had put ready placated him, and they parted on the best of terms, condoling with each other over the increasing heat. Once or twice indeed, after she had gone, Lorrigan thought he had smelt something burning, and had gone round to investigate. But everything had seemed all right.

It was certainly very hot. Standing at the door of the house for a few minutes before going upstairs to the bed that had been made up for him in Berringer's room, Lorrigan thought to himself that it was partly due to the position of the house. It lay in a much deeper hollow than he had realized, and yet he had known the road well enough for seven or eight years, ever since he had come to Smetham. He had often been along it on his motor-cycle, and he had always thought of it as mounting just past the house in a gentle rise to the slightly higher ridge where the trees were. But to-night as he stood there, looking out, it seemed very different. The hedge looked higher, and much steeper; indeed, all round the house the ground was much higher than he remembered. He looked along the road in the direction of the climbing road, and thought lazily, "It does climb too." For a wild moment, the house and Mr. Berringer and he all seemed very deep, almost at the bottom of a pit, with ground up about them like walls. There had been less thunder this last day or two, which was fortunate, for it was a creepy house he was in—and he rather wished the housekeeper had not gone. Talk was a useful thing; it kept one steady, he thought, unconsciously repeating Anthony's "It supports the wings in the air" of the previous day. And there were all sorts of little shiverings and quiverings and flickers—once or twice it had been exactly like a little flame at the edge of his eyes. Patients who felt shiverings and quiverings and saw flames and flashes he was more or less used to. He had once been male nurse for three years to an old gentleman who had a recurring belief that he had been responsible for the Great Fire of London, and who had in consequence at those times fits of deep melancholy and remorse at the deaths he had caused, accompanied by a spasmodic terror of being himself cut off by the Fire. Lorrigan's own view had been that this gentleman ought to have been put away, but the family couldn't bring themselves to such extreme measures, so he was relegated to the Dower House and Lorrigan, and books on the higher mathematics in which he was an acknowledged authority. But with all his drawbacks he had been, at his best, a pleasant gentleman, and the house had been away among the South Downs, where everything was much less oppressive. Lorrigan sighed, and went to bed.

In the morning it was, if anything, worse. The sun was blazing down, and nobody came along the road. It had never been a busy road, but it had not, when he had been along it, ever seemed so deserted as it was now. He waited impatiently for Mrs. Portman's return.

She came about half-past eleven full of the rumours that were going about the town. When he heard of the fall of the telephones Lorrigan went off to try their own, and found indeed that he could not get a reply from the Exchange at

Smetham. He came back to her rather gloomily, and inter-rupted her repetition of her story to ask if she could smell burning. "It's getting a very peculiar house, this," he said. "The old man upstairs—well, I don't mind him; I'm used to them. But all this smell of fire, and things breaking down . . . And dreams. I don't know when I've dreamt as badly as I did last night. It was a regular nightmare. All animals—you wouldn't believe, Mrs. Portman; I might have been to the Zoo. There was a great lion walking round everywhere. . . . I couldn't get past him—you know how it is in dreams . . ."

"Why," said Mrs. Portman, "would you believe it, that's what my daughter's little girl was talking about this morning. Out in the garden before breakfast she was, and came running in to say that there must be a circus come to Smetham, for she'd just seen a big lion go by the end of the garden. She couldn't talk of anything else all breakfast time till her mother shut her up, her father not being very well. He's a policeman, you know, and he'd been on night duty, and came in all dazed this morning. Couldn't talk of anything but how lovely some-things was."

"There's not much that's all that lovely," Mr. Lorrigan said pessimistically.

"O I don't know," Mrs. Portman answered. "I like a bit of colour round myself, but I'm not in it with Jack. He ought to've been a painter instead of a policeman, the things he sees in trees and sunsets. I tell him he wouldn't notice a murder right before his eyes if there was a sunset there too."

"Sunsets have their place," said Lorrigan. "Not that I've ever seen much in a sunset myself. My Bessie did an essay on sunsets the other day at school, and the things that child put in! I've not seen all those colours in a sunset—not for forty years. And anyhow I don't hold with teaching children to do too much sky gazing; there's other things that's more important."

"That's so," Mrs. Portman said, "and if I was going to buy a picture it'd be one of those that have got more to them than just a lot of different colours. I like a picture to have a story in it, something that you can enjoy. I've got one upstairs that belonged to my mother—*The Last Days of King Charles the First*, and I'm sure it used to make me cry to look at it, all so natural with the little children and everything. I tell you, Mr. Lorrigan, I like a picture that makes me feel something."

"I don't care for pictures much, anyhow," Lorrigan answered. "Though, of course, a good lifelike bit of work . . . One of the best I ever saw was the sign of an inn out the other side of the town—that was a lion too: the *Red Lion,* and anything more natural I never saw. I wonder if I got thinking of it last night."

"I expect so," Mrs. Portman said. "Lor', isn't it close, Mr. Lorrigan? I could do with a cup of tea after that walk. Will you have a cup too?"

"Well, I don't mind," Mr. Lorrigan agreed. "I'll just have another look at Mr. Berringer while you get your hat off, and then take a turn in the garden till it's ready."

"Do," Mrs. Portman said, and went off to her room. In a few minutes she was downstairs again, and went across to light the gas and put on the kettle for her tea. It would have needed Anthony's purged eyes to see then what neither she in the kitchen not Lorrigan in the garden could see—the multiplicity of intellectual flame that was leaping and twining all over the house. Some new passion was spreading out through earthly things, another Energy pressed onwards to the moment in which, concerned upon its own business, it should yet take the opportunity of whatever opening into matter might be afforded to it. Mrs. Portman picked up a box of matches, and as the invisible fire arched itself round and over her paused in amused remembrance of her granddaughter's chatter about the lion. Then she opened it, took out a match, struck it——

In the garden Lorrigan was strolling from the gate back towards the house. A wave of heat struck him, a terrific burst of fire blinded him. He reeled back, shouting incoherently, with his hands to his eyes. When he could open them again, after that violent shock, he saw before him the whole house blazing to heaven. This was no fire spreading from room to room, though his first thought was that the curtains had caught. But from the road to which he had fled, looking dazedly back, he saw not flames breaking out from doors or windows, but now a pillar, now a nest of fire. It soared, it sank, it spread outwards and curved back inwards; the heat and light of the burning struck and hurt him, and he went stumbling farther along the road to escape it. "What's happened?" he thought stupidly. "What's she done? Christ, the whole place is alight!" The roar of the fire beat in his ears; he covered them with his hands and blinked out over the fields. And then he remembered his charge.

He faced round, feeling that he ought to do something. But it was evident, even to his ruining intelligence, that nothing could be done. No one could live in that destructive ferocity of flame; both his patient and Mrs. Portman must already have perished. He had better get hold of somebody; the fire brigade, the police—and the telephones were down. Lorrigan felt like crying, his helplessness was obvious and extreme. It wasn't more than ten minutes since he had been talking to Mrs. Portman in that kitchen about pictures and lions and zoos, and now she and her master were burnt to death, and the house was falling in. . . . "O God . . ." he exclaimed, "don't let her come out," for he had had a moment's dreadful fear of some burning creature rushing out of that fiery splendour. "O God, kill her, kill her," he thought unintentionally, "and then put it out." But God went on concerning Himself with his Deity and that seemed to imply the continuation of the fire.

It was some time later that Lorrigan came racing into the town, and a shorter time later still that the fire brigade, and Dr. Rockbotham, and a number of other people were assembled round the house. So fierce was the heat that they were all kept at a good distance, and the efforts that were made to approach the house closely all failed. The hoses were turned on; streams of water were dashed against the fire. By this time it had been burning for the best part of an hour, and if anything it seemed more violent than before. "You shouldn't have left him, Lorrigan," Dr. Rockbotham exclaimed, quite unjustly, in the excitement of the moment.

"No," said Lorrigan, also excited. "I suppose I ought to have sat by him and been burnt up too. I suppose you pay me for that, don't you? I suppose . . ."

The doctor looked at him sharply. "Now steady, steady," he said. "Of course, you couldn't tell. I didn't intend to blame you. I only meant that . . ." He stopped, aware that he had as a fact meant to blame the nurse, and then resumed, "There, I apologize if I hurt you."

But Lorrigan's usual equanimity had vanished. "Coming to me and telling me I ought to have stopped there!" he said. 'What d'you mean, hey? What d'you mean?" He caught the doctor's arm, and shook it fiercely.

"Leave go at once," Rockbotham exclaimed, shaken out of his usual benignity. "How dare you touch me? Leave go!"

In the general surging of the crowd in the road a new little vortex formed around the two of them.

"Now then, Jack," a voice said, "don't you be silly."

"Ah," said another voice, "it's all very fine, blaming a man for not letting himself be burnt! There's too many treat us that way!"

The doctor looked round. It was a mixed crowd, and part of it wasn't very nice. Loafers and bullies from Smetham had been attracted by the blaze. Lorrigan still held his arm; another man drove an elbow, as if accidentally, into his side. "Take care," the doctor exclaimed.

Immediately a sudden fierceness awoke in them. They jolted, thrust, hit at him. His hat was knocked off, and his glasses. He called out. Others in the crowd heard him, looked round, saw what was happening, and came pushing in on one

side or the other. In less than five minutes after Rockbotham's
first remark nothing less than a free fight was going on. It was
not, perhaps, a serious fight, but it shook the doctor very
greatly. People were grunting and snarling at each other all
round him; they were behaving, he thought disgustedly, like
animals. A couple of constables intervened, and the row
quietened down. But though the crowd turned its attention
again to the fire the panting and grunting remained, as if
indeed some animal rather than human nature was then
dominating its members. And over everything went up the
roar of the fire.

An hour, two hours, went by. Still the hoses were directed
towards the blaze; still the torrents of water fell on it. But
when three hours were past, and more—when the afternoon
was almost done—when the crowd had changed and multiplied
and lessened and multiplied again—still the house burned. At
least, presumably it was the house. The Captain of the Fi ?
Brigade talked with the Police-Inspector, who suggested that
there might be a store of chemicals somewhere in the cellars.
Hadn't Mr. Berringer been a scientific man?

"I suppose it must be something like that," the Captain said.
"But it seems very odd."

"It's odd how the flames hide the house," the Inspector
answered. "Generally you can see the walls except for a
minute or two here and there. But here you can't see anything
but the fire. And that looks more like a great nest than anything."

"With a bird in it, I suppose," the Captain answered, looking
irritably at the blaze, and then at his watch. "Why, it's been
going on for five hours and it's as bad as ever."

"Ah, well, I daresay you'll get it under soon," the Inspector
said encouragingly, and moved off.

But when the night fell, that violent and glorious catastrophe
was still visible over the countryside. It was burning up
through the earth; indeed, the Captain found himself thinking

occasionally the base of that fiery pillar expanded, and by midnight the perplexed firemen found that its extreme circle had reached on one side to the middle of the garden, the flames seeming to rise from the ground as if the withered grass and the dry hard ground beneath broke into fire of their own accord. The increasing heat drove the workers back, such of them as were left. For a few had been overcome, and one had been almost blinded by an unexpected outbreak of crimson light, and the idle watchers had disappeared. Not merely night and weariness had drawn these off, but a vague rumour an echo of which reached the Captain himself from the mouth of one of his men.

"Did you hear they're shutting up in the town?"

"What d'you mean—shutting up?" the Captain asked.

"All the pubs are closing, they say," the man said. "There's animals going about the streets"—and he added another "they say."

"It sounds as if it was time the pubs closed," the Captain muttered. "Don't talk that blasted rubbish to me. For Christ's sake look what you're doing."

Yet his incredulity would have ceased could he have seen the town as it lay away behind him. The doors were shut, the streets were empty, a terrified populace hid in dark houses behind such protection as they could find. For now here and now there, first one and then another wayfarer had seen forms and images, and fled in terror. Certain courageous folk had heard the rumours, and mocked at them, and gone out, but by midnight these too had come rushing home, and the streets were given up to the moonlight, while all one side of the heavens was filled with the glow of the burning. Under that distant glow, and passing from the moon to the dark and from the dark to the moon, there went all night the subdued sound of mighty creatures. Sceptical eyes looked out from occasional windows, and beheld them: the enormous bulk of the Lion, the coiling smoothness of the Serpent, even, very rarely, the careering figure of the Unicorn. And above them went the never-resting flight of the Eagle, or, if indeed it rested, then it was at some moment when, soaring into its own dominion, it found a nest exalted beyond human sight in the vast mountains of the creation natural to it, where it might repose and contemplate its æonian wisdom. There among the Andes and Himalayas of the soul, it sank to rest; thence again, so swiftly it renewed its youth, it swept out, and passing upon its holy business, cast from its wings the darkness which is both mortal night and night of the mind. It knew, since it knew all things, the faint sounds of the lesser world that was more and more passing into the place of the Angelicals, but what to it were those sounds, however full of distress they might be? For, as the quivering human creatures knew, the destruction was spreading. It was no longer only neglected sheds and empty houses, posts and palisades, that were falling. An inhabited house crashed in ruins, and screams and moans broke through the night. A little after, in another part of the town, a second fell; and then a third. In the double fear that, even through those barred and shuttered houses, began to spread, there was hinted panic. Men came out to help and caught sight of something and fled, except only those who saw the silver horn and heard the silver hooves of the Angel of their Return; they only, free from fear, toiled to rescue their fellows.

All others, crouched in darkness, waited in terror for death.

Chapter Fourteen

THE HUNTING OF QUENTIN

Damaris, on that Monday morning, was conscious as she ate her breakfast of one surprising truth. She had, as a matter of fact, almost finished before the consciousness of it came upon her, though the fact itself had been with her since she woke. She sat staring at the last bit of toast on her plate, as she realized that, very surprisingly, she wasn't worrying. Until that moment it had never seemed to her that she did worry very much; other things worried her, but that was different. It was not she who fretted; it was she who was fretted. It occurred to her suddenly that of all the follies of which she had been guilty, and they seemed to have been many and stupendous, none had ever been greater than that. She had always regarded herself as an unchangeable fact, attacked and besieged by a troublesome world. But she could as easily be, indeed at the moment she was, a changeable fact, beautifully concerned with a troubled world. She had been worrying all her life about herself, and now she wasn't worrying any more. It was not perhaps possible for her then to realize that this was because she herself didn't—for the moment—exist for herself. There being for Damaris—in that moment—no Damaris, there was no Damaris for Damaris to worry about. However soon that lucid integrity might become clouded and that renewed innocence inevitably stained, it did then exist. All this she did not perhaps realize, but she did definitely feel the marvellous release. She still wanted to get on with her work—if she could, if she could approach it with this new sense that her subjects were less important than her subjects' subject, that her arrangements

167

were very tentative presentations of the experiences of great minds and souls. But work was less important than her immediate task. She ate the toast and stood up pensively. Here she was, abandoning Abelard—Abelard . . . the word had a new sound. She saw the brilliant young tonsured clerk, the crowds in the growing University, the developing intellect and culture; she felt the rush and tumult—almost physically she felt it—of the students pouring to hear him, because they were burning to listen, to learn, to . . . To learn. Damaris twiddled a fork on the table, and felt herself blushing. "The credulous piety . . ." she bit her lip. No, Abelard, St. Bernard, St. Thomas—no, they were not merely the highest form in a school of which she was the district inspector. No, intellect might make patterns, but itself it was a burning passion, a passion stronger even than that other love of Peter Abelard for Heloise, the Canon's niece, which had always seemed to her a pity—a pity not merely for Abelard himself but in general. To learn. Well, she wasn't past learning, thank God. If it had all got to be redone, it should be redone. Anything should be done that fitted in with Anthony and the sunlight and freedom from worry and that stranger thing which she dimly realized had been the central desire of centuries of labour. But to-morrow. To-day there was Quentin.

She went into the kitchen and made herself some sandwiches, considerably to the maid's astonishment. She even attempted a little conversation, but she was feeling so shy that it was not altogether a success. The maid, she realized, was very much on her guard. That was the kind of world that Damaris Tighe had hitherto insisted on making all round her, a world where people were watchful and hostile. She looked at it humbly while she finished the sandwiches; then she went upstairs to her father.

He hadn't come down to breakfast for the last two days, and the tray that had been taken up to him stood on a table by the bed. But it was with a shock that she realized that he had not even undressed. He had laid down the night before, and though she called out good night to him she had not gone in. For here again was the opposition she had created, and she felt shy and distressed about it. But not worried—not nearly as worried over this far more serious thing as she had been so lately about his apparent disturbance of her work. Or what she chose to think a disturbance. No, not worried. If this also had to be done again, well, it had to be done, that was all. There seemed to be quite a lot that looked like having to be done over again. Everything perhaps except—she realized it as she crossed the room—except Anthony. But she had treated Anthony as she had these others. Well, it was a pity, but something was present there which touched even that iniquity with laughter and holy delight and sweet irony, so that—if Anthony would—they might smile at it together. In a delicate gratitude she came to her father.

He was lying with his eyes shut, motionless. The breakfast tray was untouched. She leaned over him, touched him, spoke to him, and very slowly he opened his eyes, but they did not seem to see her. They did not seem to see anything; their vision was awfully withdrawn. Damaris sank down by the bed, looking at him in fear, but it was with nothing of the same fear as she had experienced on the previous night. She was in the presence of some process which she did not understand, and of which she stood in awe, but she was not merely afraid of it. "Father," she said softly, and a flicker of recognition came into his eyes. He moved his lips; she leant nearer. "Glory," he said, "glory," and ceased. "Can I do anything?" she asked still softly, and added with a rush of willingness to serve, "anything at all?" He moved his hand a little and she took it in her own; after a little he said, and she only just caught the words: "You weren't hurt?"

"Not much," she answered. "You and Anthony helped me." There was another long pause, then he uttered—"Not me;

169

Anthony knows.—I saw he knew—when he came.—I don't know—much. Only—this. You'll go—your way."

"I shall go," she said, and as she spoke she saw him for what seemed the first time. The absurd little man, of whom she had been ashamed, with whom she had been so irritated, on whom she had so often loosed her disguised contempt, was transfigured. He became beautiful before her; he lay there, in all his ridiculous modern clothes, and neither he nor they were at all ridiculous. The colours and tints harmonized perfectly; the slight movements he made were exquisitely proportioned and gracious; the worship that glowed full in his eyes lifted him into the company of the gods he seemed to see. Beauty adored beauty; and lay absorbed in its contemplation. Tears came into her eyes as, from a great distance, she looked at that transfiguration. He was upon his way, and she must follow hers. She felt the call within her; if she could not serve him then she must do what she could do. There was another in greater need, and salvation must be communicated or it would be lost. She might, the day before, have left him as she was about to leave him now, but then it would have been in order, grudging him even those few minutes of attention, to dash back to herself. She thought of it and was ashamed; very faintly there came to her upon the air the slightest memory of the odour of corruption. She kissed him and stood up. He smiled a little, and murmured: "Don't—get hurt,—good-bye." She kissed him again, pressed his hand, saw his eyes again close, and went.

It occurred to her, as she changed her shoes, that the maid would think she certainly ought to stop at home. Damaris shook her head helplessly: that, she supposed, was the maid's business. She could hardly expect to have the most favourable construction put on her own words and actions, but what had got to be done had got to be. Anyhow, in this case the maid was wrong. Standing up, Damaris realized that interpretations nearly always are wrong; interpretations in the nature of things being peculiarly personal and limited. The act was personal but infinite, the reasoned meaning was personal and finite. Interpretation of infinity by the finite was pretty certain to be wrong. The thought threw a light on her occupation with philosophies. Philosophy to Plato, to Abelard, to St. Thomas, was an act—the love of wisdom; to her——

But all that was to come. Love or wisdom, her act awaited her. She ran lightly down the stairs.

Neither love nor wisdom had suggested either to her or to Anthony when they had been talking whereabouts in the neighbourhood Quentin was likely to be found. Both of them indeed realized that he might not be in the neighbourhood at all. Only then, if his brain were still functioning he would probably make for the rooms in London; and if not, if fright had possessed him entirely, well, then, he might be anywhere. He might, of course, be dead, overwhelmed by the strength of the Lion, or driven by his fear to destruction. But this Anthony had doubted, on what seemed to Damaris the perfectly satisfactory grounds that, if Quentin were dead, he himself would not still feel the necessity of finding him. "It's more important even than he is," Anthony had said, frowning, "or let's say as important. There are two things muddled up— Quentin's one, and I'm not clear what the other is. But we shall be."

"We?" she asked.

"We," he answered. "Darling, that's why—that's partly why—I think you're right to go."

On the whole, then, Damaris saw no better idea than to go out to where she had had her first encounter with the young man, and then—then go whichever way suggested itself. She swung along, keeping a sharp look-out as she went; but within her her soul kept another watch, and her eyes, as they searched the hedges, were prepared both for Quentin and for some other sight. She could not tell whether the incredible visions that had manifested would show themselves to her; she

did not desire but neither would she avoid them. She permitted herself to savour, to enjoy, the sensation of trust and
dependence, and was astonished to find how comforting it was.
It was quite impossible for her to balance and equate great
Ideas, but if there were among them one whose nature was
precisely that balance and therefore the freedom of assured
movement, then she would give herself to it, whether in looking
up references about Pythagoras or looking out for Quentin
along country roads. The one thing she had no longer to do
was to look after herself. There was something that knew—
that was philosophy. Philosophy, then, she mused as she went
along, was not so much an act as a being, and it was upon those
eagle wings that all her masters had travelled. And Sophia
itself—Holy Wisdom—but she was content not to inquire
more; she would find that out when she had practised loving it
a little longer. She had wasted a lot of time, she thought, and
found herself whistling softly as her mind recalled the headings
of her papers—*The Eidola and the Angeli, Platonic Tradition at
the Court of Charlemagne*—"Damaristic tradition at the Court
of Damaris"—she laughed out. How right Anthony had
been!

She had come to Saturday's meeting-place. There was the
stile; there was the ditch; there she had gone sprawling. In a
sudden appreciation she went round to the exact spot where
Quentin had pulled her down, and stepping into the ditch
sat down where she had fallen. Quentin in his wildness had yet
kept some thought for others; he had wished to help her because she was his friend's friend—because she was Anthony's
girl. Well, if Anthony's girl could now be any use to him, who
in his madness had been greater than she in her sanity, here
she was! She sat for a moment attentive, then she sprang to
her feet. Far and fast there came to her the sound of something
galloping. That sound had echoed through her last night when
Anthony came to her, and now she heard it again. She ran up
to the stile, looked all round, saw nothing, and jumped up on

the step to see better. At a good distance away, down the steep slope beneath her, she saw *The Joinings*. Her eyes dwelled on it thoughtfully, and then very high in the air above it she saw again such a shape as had sat on Anthony's shoulder when he came to her, exalted in the secure knowledge of its nature over the offices of its peers—the idea of wisdom, the image of philosophy, the temporal extension of divine science. She stood gazing, and forgetful of her immediate business; and she was taught her duty on the instant. In the old unhappy days she had been left to herself—loving herself she was abandoned to herself. But in loving others, or seeking to love others, the great Angelicals took her in their charge. The noise of hooves rang on the road behind her; a terrible blow, as she turned, caught her shoulder and sent her flying into the hedge, and as she fell she saw a form which seemed like a silver horse, but of whose nature Richardson could have told her truer things, go galloping across the field. "Idiot!" she exclaimed cheerfully to herself, then, bruised, scratched, and aching, scrambled up, back to the stile and over it. She would follow as far as she could; perhaps this was a guide, and if not, then as well this way as any other. But how stupid of her, she thought as she tried to run, to be caught gaping like that when she had a job to do. They were a little severe, these new masters of hers. Anthony had told her of the sudden stab in his side that had warned him to be silent, and she supposed the bruise on her shoulder was to teach her to be alert. No doubt she needed it. Certainly there had been an invasion of the court of Damaris, and it was no easy conqueror that sat upon her relinquished throne.

She jumped over another stile, came into a wide meadow, and paused. The galloping form had vanished. And now what? The question was answered almost before she had framed it. There were running along the farther edge of the meadow, two figures—the first certainly a man; the second— the second a man too, she supposed, only she couldn't make

out whether it were going on two feet or four; sometimes one
and sometimes the other, it seemed. But that didn't matter; it
was the first figure to which she looked, for she knew within
her that it was Quentin.

She began to run towards them across the meadow, forget-
ting her shoulder. It was an empty meadow, at least almost
empty: there was a single white splodge, a sheep or a lamb or
something in the middle, moving gently about. But the two
figures were running much quicker than she could; she paused,
anxiously waiting to see which way they would go. If there
were a gate at the bottom. . . . But apparently there was not;
for Quentin turned at the corner and came driving up the
side. There was, she could see, no way out from that point
till he reached the stile by which she had entered; she went
back to it, and waited. They were going terribly fast, both of
them, and as they drew nearer she stared at them in horror and
pity, though not—no, never again—in fear. For Quentin,
though he was running, had already passed, it seemed to her,
any state in which a man could be, and live. He was almost
naked, he was torn and bleeding all over, especially his feet,
which appeared to her no longer feet but broken and shapeless
masses of bloody flesh. His arms were tossing frenziedly, his
hands dangling from them as they were flung about; his face
was inhuman with terror and anguish. The dreadful noise
that came to her as he drew near was his breath wrenched
from the very extreme of existence; his eyes were sightless, and
one cheek was horribly bitten and gnawed. She ran out to meet
him, tears on her face for very distress of love, and held out her
hands, and called him by both his names: "Quentin! Quentin!
Mr. Sabot! Quentin!" He did not hear or see her; he rushed
on, past her, past the stile, round the meadow; and while she
cried to him the second form was near her. It too was going
swiftly; but it still seemed to be rather leaping than running.
Its clothing also was part gone and part disordered; but its
boots were on its feet, and its arms not tossing but held close

to it, with crooked fingers. The face was as inhuman as that
other, but while that was man blasted this was man brutalized.
It was a snarling animal, and it was snuffling and snorting with
open mouth. Yet she had a dreadful feeling of recognition; she
could find no name for it, but somewhere it had had a name,
somewhere in her own past it also had had a past, and that
past was appallingly kindred to the horror she had seen on the
evening before. All this she took in as it came up to her, and
sprang forward, greatly adventuring, to check or distract or
fight it. Vainly; as she moved a wind poured from its passage
and flung her backward till she reeled against the stile. There
was strength in and about the man, if it were a man, that drove
her from him; or the beast, if it were a beast, for as again she
went forward and looked after him, he had lost his upright
position, and was leaping clumsily forward, if not actually on
all fours, yet so bent and thrust forward that he seemed altogether more animal than human. She ran out into the meadow,
and paused; the chase was now going down the fourth side.
Since she could not prevent the pursuit she might perhaps aid
the pursued. But how? how?

Willing to do all but uncertain what to do, she watched, and
then became aware of some other thing in her line of vision.
It was the solitary lamb that was gently moving towards her,
gently and slowly. She looked at it, and across the meadow
there passed suddenly the shadow of the flying eagle, cast over
her and proceeding from her towards the lamb. Moved by a
quick hope she followed it; the beast, more slowly, advanced
to meet her. They came together, and the innocence that
sprang in her knew a greater innocence and harmlessness in
it; she dropped to her knees, and put a hand on its back. So
kneeling, she looked again at that terrible hunt, which, though
she did not then know it, had already been going on for several
hours. It had been close after midnight when, wandering out
of the town upon his greedy pursuit of prey, the creature that
had been Foster had startled Quentin from uneasy sleep in the

bracken, had scented and trailed him, and once, when Quentin had stumbled and fallen, had come up with and worried him. But the extreme madness of fear had given Quentin strength enough to make one wild struggle, and he had escaped. After that, through the night and the dawn and the early morning, the hunt had gone on, through lanes and woods and fields, now swiftly, now slowly. Sometimes after crossing a small river or among thick trees the driven wretch had had a few minutes respite, but always sooner or later the inevitable snuffling and trampling had drawn near, and again the flight had begun. Quentin now was beginning to run merely round and round; only as he fled along the meadow side once more, something came crying to what function of his brain was left. Damaris, kneeling by the lamb, went on calling—calling one name alone, steadily, clearly, entreatingly—"Quentin! Quentin! Quentin!" She saw his head turn a little, and renewed her effort. He wavered; the creature behind was almost on him. He broke inward across the meadow, and still the voice of Damaris sounded to guide him, though what she was to do when he came she did not know. He came; he was with them; right before her he flung his arms wide once more and fell, and she threw herself forward over his body to protect and guard it with her own. At the feet of the lamb they lay, and the pursuing creature gave vent to something that was both laugh and snarl, and paused, and very softly began to creep round them before he sprang. Damaris thought of several things at once—Anthony and the Eagle and her father, but all of them vanished in the flood of simplicity that suddenly took her. For some reason she knew assuredly that the thing would not hurt her; its hate and its power divided and passed round her. She leaned over Quentin, looking into his sightless eyes, searching him with no purpose but to find what secret of life still throve in him and, for what she could, to nourish it. And by them both, frisking in the sunlight, the lamb jumped and ran and rested and gave itself up to joy.

The Hunting of Quentin

The other creature continued its uneasy perambulation. As it went circling round them it uttered little noises of effort and pain. Sometimes it made a sudden abrupt rush inward, but every rush was diverted from its intended prey; it was, against its will, drawn aside, and thrust back into its own path. The lamb took no notice of it whatever; Damaris glanced up at it occasionally, but with a serene absent-mindedness; Quentin lay still, his hand in the woman's, while with her other she tried, with her handkerchief and a fragment torn from her dress, to wipe away the drying blood from his face. But suddenly there pierced through this passion of goodwill a long and dreadful howl. She looked up. The thing that had pursued them was farther away, and was, apparently by some interior power, being drawn still farther. It was retreating, slowly and grotesquely, and she saw as she looked that under it the grass was all leaning one way as if blown by a wind. With that wind the creature was struggling; it was lifted a little, and hung absurdly in the air, an inch or two off the ground, then it fell and sprawled full length and twisted and howled. She looked over her shoulder; the lamb was cropping the grass. She looked at Quentin; repose was coming back into his face, and with it that beauty of innocence which is seen in unhappy mankind only in sleep and death and love and transmuting sanctity— the place of the lamb in the place of the lion.

Within that farther place Damaris rested. But without, that which had once been the intelligent and respected Mr. Foster struggled to control the strength which he could no longer control. For a few days he had, even with the Idea, exercised some kind of domination upon the Idea, but as the earth, and he with it, slipped more deeply into that other state of being, his poor personal desire could no longer govern or separate. That which was in him rushed to mingle with that which was without. The power of the Lion came upon him in a great wind, and the breath of his spirit fled to meet it. Strangled and twisted, he was lifted and carried on the wind; he was flung into the air and carelessly dropped back on to the earth. As he fell for that last time he saw the Lion upon him. The giant head loomed over him; the great paw struck his chest and thrust him down. Immense pressure enclosed and crushed him; in a dreadful pain he ceased to be.

Damaris, glancing up with a start of recollection from the Lamb and Quentin, looked round for their enemy. It was not for some minutes that she saw, away in the meadow, crushed and trodden flat, and driven by that treading right into the earth, the body of a man.

Even then it was to her no more than fact. She stood up and looked again to be certain, then she turned her perplexed attention to Quentin. It was by no means clear to her that if she left him he would not go rushing off again, yet she could not get him to the town without help. She paused uncertainly; then she decided at least to try. She bent down and slipped her arm under his shoulders; with something of an effort she half raised him.

He seemed to be vaguely conscious; murmuring encouragement she got him to his feet, and, moving very slowly, managed to make him take an uncertain step forward. It pierced her heart to persist in his using those terrible bleeding feet; she had drawn one arm over her shoulders, and as much as possible relieved them of his weight. Even so the pain troubled his wandering mind, and his body moaned under its suffering. But this she had to ignore. Very, very slowly, they crossed the meadow and reached the stile, and as they did so he came to himself enough to understand something of what was happening. So concentrated was she on this concern that she did not notice the blaze that broke out from the house in the distance below; she had to get him over the stile.

It was by then midday. She would have left him then, had she dared and could she, to find some car, but he would not let her go. Her efforts at explanation he understood but rejected; she was to keep with him, he made clear, and he would do his best to get along. So, all through that long hot afternoon, both the man and the woman retraced their steps along the hard country road—Quentin from his flight, Damaris from her seclusion—and came at last to the house where, as twilight began to fall, her father drew his last breath in final surrender to the beauty that had possessed him.

Chapter Fifteen

THE PLACE OF FRIENDSHIP

Anthony opened the door of the flat and went quickly into it. He called out as he did so, not that he had much hope of an answer, even if Quentin were there. But instinctively his voice went before him, desiring to cry out to that wilderness of spirit, to proclaim the making straight of the highway of God. No other replied.

He went into each room, and even looked behind chairs and inside a deep cupboard or two and under tables and beds. The agonized fugitive might so easily have tried to hide himself in such an absurd refuge. But he had not; after a very few minutes Anthony was compelled to admit that the flat was untenanted. He came back into their common lounge and sat down. Quentin wasn't here; then he was still in flight—or helpless, or dead. The first possibility of the two which had been in Anthony's mind—that of finding his friend—had proved useless; the second and less defined—the hinted discovery in this house of friendship of a means of being of use to the troubled world—remained. He lay back in his chair and let his eyes wander round the room.

The traces of their common occupation lay before him, rather tidier at this hour of the morning than they generally were, because the woman who looked after the flat had obviously only just "been round it" and gone. She had been broken of her original habit of putting everything straight, of thrusting papers away in drawers and pushing books back on to shelves—any book on any shelf, so that Spinoza and Mr. T. S. Eliot might jostle, which would have been quite suitable, but then also Milton might neighbour a study in Minoan

origins, which was merely inconvenient, or Mr. Gerard
Hopkins shoulder Mr. Gilbert Frankau, which was silly. So
books and papers—and even pipes—still lay on tables, and
Quentin's fountain-pen upon a pile of letter-paper. There were
the pictures, most of them signs of some memory—this of a
common holiday, that of a common friend, that again of a
birthday or even of a prolonged argument. A little reproduc-
tion of Landseer's *Monarch of the Glen* was the sign of the last.
Anthony had forgotten for the moment what the terrific discussion had really been about, though he knew in general
terms that it was on the nature of art and had arisen out of a
review of his own in *The Two Camps*. But he remembered how
Quentin had won a perfectly devastating triumph, and how
the next day he had himself searched several picture shops to
find the Landseer and had triumphantly presented it to
Quentin that evening as a commemoration of the battle and
in illustration of the other's principles. Or so he swore it was,
though Quentin had rampantly denied it; but they had hung
the thing up in mutual laughter, derision, and joy. Anthony's
eyes left it reluctantly, and went on glancing round the room.

The moments of their past showed themselves multitudinously to him as he looked. In that chair Quentin had sat
sprawled on a winter evening, while he himself, pacing up and
down the warm unlit room, had delivered a long monologue
on Damaris; in yonder corner he had himself crouched with
books scattered round him while they disputed which "chorus-
ending from Euripides" might conceivably have been in
Browning's mind. Quentin had a fantastic passion for discovering impossible suitabilities. By the window they had both
leaned one evening, while they talked of the exact kind of
authority which reposed in moments of exalted experience and
how far they each sought to obey it. In another chair they had
once seated an uneasy canvasser before a general election, and
plied him with questions and epigrams about the nature of the
State, and whether a dictatorship was consistent with the

English political genius. By the table they had once nearly quarrelled; near the fireplace they had read immortal verse from a new illustrated edition of *Macbeth* which had come to Anthony for review, and had been propped up on the mantelpiece for admiration. Light and amusing, poignant and awful, the different hours of friendship came to him, each full of that suggestion of significance which hours of the kind mysteriously hold—a suggestion which demands definitely either to be accepted as truth or rejected as illusion. Anthony had long since determined on which side his own choice lay; he had accepted those exchanges, so far as mortal frailty could, as being of the nature of final and eternal being. Though they did not last, their importance did; though any friendship might be shattered, no strife and no separation could deny the truth within it: all immortality could but more clearly reveal what in those moments had been.

More certainly than ever he now believed. He reaccepted what they offered; he reaccepted *them*, knowing from of old that this, which seems so simple, is one of the hardest tasks laid before mankind. Hard, for the reality is so evasive; self-consciousness, egotism, heaviness, solemnity, carelessness, even an over-personal fondness, continually miss it. He could do nothing but indicate to that fleeting truth his willingness to be at its service. It accepted him in turn; it renewed within him its work of illumination. He felt how some moving power bore Quentin and himself within it, and so bearing them passed onward through time. Or perhaps it *was* Time; in that they were related, and outside that there was only . . . whatever "the perfect and simultaneous possession of everlasting life" might be. The phrase, he remembered, came from St. Thomas; perhaps Damaris would once have quoted it in a footnote.

He sat on, from recollection passing to reflection, from reflection to obedience, from obedience into a trance of attention. As he had dreamed, if it were a dream, that he rose on powerful wings through the air of the spiritual abyss, so now he felt again the power between Quentin and himself active in its own place. Within that power the presence of his friend grew more defined to him, and the room in which he sat was but the visible extension of an immortal state. He loved; yet not he, but Love living in him. Quentin was surely there, in the room, leaning by the window as he had so often leaned, and Anthony instinctively rose and went across, as he had so often gone across, to join him. If, when he reached it, there was no mortal form, there was yet a reception of him into something that had been and still was; his movement freed it to make a movement of its own. He stood and looked out of the window upon the world.

It presented itself to him in an apparition of strength. How firmly the houses were set within the ground! with what decision each row of bricks lay level upon the row beneath! Spires and towers and chimneys thrust into the sky, and slender as they were, it was an energetic slenderness. The trees were drawing up strength and displaying it, and the sunlight communicated strength. The noises that came to him from the streets resolved themselves into a litany of energy. Matter was directed by and inspired with this first and necessary virtue, and through the vast spaces of the sky potential energy expanded in an azure wonder.

But the sounds that came to him, though they reached him as a choric hymn, sounding almost like the subdued and harmonious thunder of the lion's roar, were yet many. A subtlety of music held them together, and the strength whose epiphany was before him was also subtilized into its complex existence. Neither virtue could exist without the other: the slender spires were a token of that unison. What intelligence, what cunning, what practice, had gone to build them! Even the chimneys— ways for smoke, improvements on the mere holes by which the accidents of fire dispersed—and fire itself, all signs of man's invention! He, as he stood there, was an incredibly subtle creation, nerves, sinews, bones, muscle, skin and flesh, heart

183

and a thousand organs and vessels. They were his strength, yet his strength parcelled and ordered according to many curious divisions, even as by a similar process of infinite change the few clouds that floated in the sky were transmuted from and into rivers and seas. The seas, the world itself, was a mass of subtle life, existing only by means of those two vast Principles—and the stars beyond the world. For through space the serpentine imagination coiled and uncoiled in a myriad shapes, at each moment so and not otherwise, and the next moment entirely different and yet so and not otherwise again.

The Lion and the Serpent—but what arose between them, the first visitant from the world of abstract knowledge, the blue of the sky, the red of the bricks, the slenderness of the spires? "The world was created by number," someone had said—Pythagoras, of course. Dear Damaris! But when Number came to man, it was shown, not merely in pure intellectual proportions, which were no doubt more like its own august nature—No, they weren't; why were mathematics more after its nature than butterflies? Beauty went with strength and subtlety, and made haste to emotion as to mind, to sense as to spirit. One and indivisible, those three mighty Splendours yet offered themselves each to other—and had a fourth property also, and that was speed.

He stood there, looking out, and as if from some point high in space he beheld the world turning on its axis and at the same time rushing forward. So also he looked on created things and saw them moving rapidly upon their own concerns yet also moving forward in a unity. Within the sunlight he could almost have believed that a herd of wild horses came charging towards him across "the savannahs of the blue," only they were not a herd and not coming towards him; they were single and going from him, or would have been had he not been following at a similar speed. And now the trance deepened upon him, and what had before been half deliberate thought was now dream or vision—and, as if for the last time, he felt the choice offered him once more. Moments of love were either reality or illusion; the instant knowledge required his similar decision. He made it at once, and the sunlight grew brighter still and flowed through and around him. Quentin was leaning on the other side of the window, or whatever opening it was, in whatever world, through which the light poured, and more than light. For the light changed as he remembered again that it was not Quentin but the thing that was between him and Quentin, the thing that went with speed, and yet, speeding, was already at its goal, the thing that was for ever new and for ever old—*tam antiqua, tam nova*, that issued from its own ardent nest in its own perpetually renovated beauty, a rosy glow, a living body, the wonder of earthly love. The movement of the Eagle was the measure of truth, but the birth of some other being was the life of truth, some other royal creature that rose from fire and plunged into fire, momently consumed, momently reborn. Such was the inmost life of the universe, infinitely destroyed, infinitely recreated, breaking from its continual death into continual life, instinct with strength and subtlety and beauty and speed. But the blazing Phœnix lived and swept again to its nest of fire, and as it sank all those other Virtues went with it, themselves still, yet changed. The outer was with the inner; the inner with the outer. All of them rose in the Phœnix and a pattern of stars shone round its head, for the interfused Virtues made a pattern of worlds and stayed, and all the worlds lived and brought forth living creatures to cry out one moment for joy and then be swallowed in the Return. Ephemera of eternity, they broke into being, and Quentin who stood opposite him was one of them, and Damaris was another, and the song of joy filled them and swept them down as it pulsed for sheer gladness into silence again. But the red glow was changing; a soft white light was substituting itself, in the midst of which there grew the form of a Lamb. It stood quietly, and by it he saw Quentin lying on the ground and Damaris leaning over him. They were in some open place, and around them in circling haste went the Lion, and circling within its path, but in the opposite direction, leapt the Lamb. He saw the concentric and complementary paths only for a moment, for his attention rested on a point between Damaris and Quentin, a point that was speeding infinitely away from them, so that his own gaze passed between, and they were on each side of him, and then they were not. The point hung in remote space.

It hung, and after many centuries it opened out, floating nearer, and within it was the earth itself. That which had been but a point resolved itself into a web of speeding and interwoven colours of so many tones that he could but recognize one here and there. He saw a golden Lion against that background, and again a Butterfly of sprinkled azure, and a crimson Phœnix and a white Lamb, and others which he could not know, so swift were the transmutations. But always the earth—already he could distinguish it, with masses of piling waters heaped back from the dry land between—was in the very forefront of whatever creature showed itself. Presently it hid them altogether, hid even the web of colour, though very dimly within it he could still see the pulsations of the glories. They were not to be denied; they thrust out from it; darkened and in strange shapes. If he had been among them—some million-year-old memory woke in his brain—*when* he had been among them, with undeveloped brain and hardly lit spirit, they had gone about him as terrifying enemies—the pterodactyl and the dinosaur, Behemoth and Leviathan. It was not until man began to know them by the spiritual intellect that they were minimized to his outer sight; it was to those who were in process of degrading intellect and spirit that, mentally or actually, they appeared again, in those old, huge, and violent shapes. When the holy imagination could behold them in forms yet nearer their true selves, even the present animal appearances would disappear; the Angelicals would be known as Angelicals, and in the idea of Man all ideas would be at one: then man would know himself. For then the Lion would not be without the Lamb. It was the Lamb of which he was again aware, aware vaguely of Damaris and Quentin somewhere at hand. His thought returned to his friend. Was Quentin to be exposed already to the full blast of those energies? what were Damaris and he doing but trying to redeem him from them? Nay, what else had he been trying to do for Damaris herself? Some dispensation of the Mercy had used him for that purpose, to moderate, by the assumption of his natural mind into living knowledge, the danger that threatened his lover and his friend.

His friend. The many moments of joy and deep content which their room had held had in them something of the nature of holy innocence. There had been something in them which was imparted, by Love to love, and which had willed to save them now. Much was possible to a man in solitude; perhaps the final transmutations and achievements in the zones on the yonder side of the central Knowledge were possible only to the spirit in solitude. But some things were possible only to a man in companionship, and of these the most important was balance. No mind was so good that it did not need another mind to counter and equal it, and to save it from conceit and blindness and bigotry and folly. Only in such a balance could humility be found, humility which was a lucid speed to welcome lucidity whenever and wherever it presented itself. How much he owed to Quentin! how much—not pride but delight urged the admission—Quentin owed to him! Balance—and movement in balance, as an eagle sails up on the wind—this was the truth of life, and beauty in life.

But if so—and unconsciously he turned now from the window and wandered back through that place of friendship to the chair he most commonly used—if so, what of the world of men under this visitation? He thought first of Damaris's father, but also of the struggle in Dora Wilmot's house. One was in some sense beautiful—the other had been horrible; but even that first entire submission and absorption, was it quite the perfect end? This abandonment, awe-inspiring as it had been, surely lacked something; would the great classic poets have desired it for a conclusion? If man was perfectly to know. . . . And if Mr. Tighe had subordinated himself to one Idea, were not those others in process of being subordinated, each by an Idea to itself? And for others still, what awaited them but thunder, earthquake, terror, chaos—the destruction of patterns and the blasting of purposes?

Unthinkingly he put out his hand to the cigarette box which Quentin had given him one Christmas; given both of them, as he had himself pointed out, in remarking on the superior nature of his own present, which had been a neat kind of pocket-book and therefore an entirely personal gift. But Quentin had maintained that the cigarette box, as being of greater good to a greater number, had been nearer to the ideal perfection of giving. "For", he had argued, "to give to you a means by which you can give to others, is better than to give a merely private thing."

"But", Anthony had persisted, "in so far as you are one of those others—and likely to be the most persistent—you give to yourself and therefore altogether deprive the act of the principle of giving"; to which Quentin had retorted that he was included only as one of a number, and that the wise man would not deprive others of good because he himself might be a gainer. "Otherwise what about all martyrs, missionaries, and philanthropists?" And so the comedy had been played to its end.

The comedy—but this was no comedy; the fierceness of the Lion was no comedy, nor any of those other apparitions, unless the Lamb . . . The Lion and the Lamb—and a little child shall lead them. Lead them where? Even a little child was in its own mind presumably leading them somewhere. Or perhaps not, perhaps a little child would be content just to lead. The Lion and the Lamb—if this were the restored balance? Friendship—love—had something in it at once strong and innocent,

The Place of Friendship

leonine and lamblike. By friendship, by love, these great
Virtues became delicately known. Apart from such love and
friendship they were merely destructive and helpless; man was
never meant to be subjected to them, unless by the offering up
of his being to "divine Philosophy." In that very chair he had
been mocked by Foster for hoping to rule the principles of
creation, and he had answered that he had promised to do
everything to help Damaris. How far such a profound intention
sufficed to rule those principles he did not know—more perhaps
than man normally thought. The balance in things—the Lion
and the Lamb, the Serpent and the Phœnix, the Horse and the
Unicorn: ideas as they were visualized and imagined—if these
could be led . . . if . . .

He could not clearly understand what suggestion was being
made to him. But an intense apprehension of the danger in
which many besides Quentin were grew within him, a danger
brought about by the disorder which had been introduced. He
could not honestly say that in any sense he loved these others,
unless indeed love were partly a process of willing good to them.
That he was determined to do, and perhaps this willing of good
meant restoration. By order man ascended; what was it that
St. Francis had written? "Set Love in order, thou that lovest
Me." First for Quentin and then for all the rest.

So gradually abandoning himself to the purpose of the great
Power that lived in him, he sat on. If the Eagle was to be served
the Eagle must show him how to serve. In this place of friendship, among the expositions and symbols of friendship, he was
filled with the intention of friendship. Quentin was not here,
but here they had been received by the knowledge of good, by
comparison with which only evil could be known. Friendship
was one, but friends were many; the idea was one, but its
epiphanies many. One winged creature—but many, many
flights of birds. The sparrows in the garden outside his window
—and the brown thrushes that sought in it sometimes—the
blackbird and the starling—the pigeons of the Guildhall and

the gulls of the Thames—the pelicans of St. James and the ridiculous penguins of the Zoo—herons in shallow waters—owls screaming by night—nightingales, skylarks, robin redbreasts—a kingfisher out beyond Maidenhead—doves and crows—ravens—the hooded falcons of pageantry—pheasants —peacocks magnificently scornful—migrating swallows of October—migrating—migrating—birds of paradise—parrots skrieking in the jungles of India—vultures tearing the bodies in the sands of Africa—flight after flight went by. He knew them in the spiritual intellect, and beheld by their fashioned material bodies the mercy which hid in matter the else overwhelming ardours; man was not yet capable of naked vision. The breach between mankind and the angelicals must be closed again; "a little child should lead them"—back. The lion should lie down with the lamb. Separately they had issued—strength divorced from innocence, fierceness from joy. They must go back together; somehow they must be called. Adam, long since—so the fable ran—standing in Eden had named the Celestials which were brought into existence before him. Their names—how should Anthony Durrant know their names, or by what title to summon again the lion and the serpent? Yet even in Anthony Durrant the nature of Adam lived. In Adam there had been perfect balance, perfect proportion: in Anthony——?

He was lying back, very still, in his chair. His desire went inwards, through a universe of peace, and hovered, as if on aquiline pinions, over the moment when man knew and named the powers of which he was made. Vast landscapes opened beneath him; laughter rang up towards him. Among the forests he saw a great glade, and in the glade wandered a solitary lamb. It was alone—for a moment or for many years; and then from the trees there came forth a human figure and stood also in the sun. With its appearance a mighty movement everywhere began. A morning of Light was on the earth; the hippopotamus lumbered from the river, the boar charged from the forest, the great apes swung down to the ground before a figure of strength and beauty, the young and glorious archetype of humanity. A voice, crying out in song, went through the air of Eden, a voice that swept up as the eagle, and with every call renewed its youth. All music was the scattered echo of that voice; all poetry was the approach of the fallen understanding to that unfallen meaning. All things were named—all but man himself, then the sleep fell upon the Adam, and in that first sleep he strove to utter his name, and as he strove he was divided and woke to find humanity doubled. The name of mankind was in neither voice but in both; the knowledge of the name and its utterance was in the perpetual interchange of love. Whoever denied that austere godhead, wherever and however it appeared—its presence, its austerity, its divinity— refused the name of man.

The echo of that high spiritual mastery sounded through the inmost being of the child of Adam who lay tranced and attentive. His memory could not bear the task of holding the sounds, but it was not memory's business. The great affair of the naming was present within him, eternal, now as much as then, and at any future hour as much as now. There floated from that singing rapture of man's knowledge of man a last note which rose through his whole being, and as it came brought with it a cloud. "A mist went up and covered the face of the earth." His faculties relaxed; his attention was gently released. He blinked once or twice, moved, saw, recognized, and drowsily smiled at the Landseer; then his head dropped down, and he was received, until his energies were renewed, into such a sleep as possessed our father when he awaited the discovery of himself.

Chapter Sixteen

THE NAMING OF THE BEASTS

The railway station at Smetham lay some half-mile out of the actual town, though it was connected by a row of houses and shops. The staff, therefore, though they soon heard whispers of strange things in the town, were still at work when Anthony, late in the evening, returned. He had spent the afternoon at his rooms in solitude and meditation and had then, rather to his own surprise, determined suddenly to go and have a good dinner. After this he had made his way to King's Cross, and got out of the train at Smetham about half-past nine. His room at the hotel was still kept for him, but he wanted first of all to see Damaris. From the station, however, he telephoned to the hotel to know if there were any messages. He was told that a gentleman was at that very moment waiting for him.

"Ask the gentleman to speak," Anthony said, and in a minute heard Richardson's voice.

"Hallo," it said. "That you, Durrant?"

"Rather," Anthony answered. "How are things with you?"

"I don't know that they are," the voice said. "Things, I mean. There seem a good many fewer, and anyhow I want to push one of them off on to you."

"Sweet of you," said Anthony cheerfully. "What particular?"

"I don't quite know", Richardson said, "what may happen, though I know what, by God's extreme mercy, I hope. But there's this book of Berringer's—you know, *Marcellus noster*—it seems the kind of thing that might be more useful to you than to me, if anyone comes at all . . ."

"O we're all coming through," Anthony interrupted. "Business as usual. Premises will be re-opened to-morrow with improvements of all kinds. But not, I fear, under entirely new management. The old isn't better, but it can't be shifted yet."

"Can't it?" the other voice said, grimly. "Well, never mind. You think things will be restored, do you?"

"The way of the world," Anthony said. "We shall jolly well have to go on making the best of both. 'Vague half-believers' —not but what Arnold himself was a bit vague."

"O stop this cultural chat," Richardson broke in, but not ill-naturedly. "I want to give you this book."

"But why?" Anthony asked. "Wasn't it you it was lent to?"

"It was," Richardson said, "but I have to be about my Father's business, and it's the only thing I've got that I ought to do anything with. Where are you? And what are you doing?"

"I'm at the station," Anthony told him, "and I'm going straight to Miss Tighe. You might come and meet me, if you've time. Where is the necessity taking you?"

There was a brief silence as if Richardson was considering; then he said, "Very well, I will. Don't walk too quickly. I'm in rather a hurry and I don't want to miss you."

"Right," said Anthony. "I'll walk like a—like the opposite of the Divine Horse till I see you. Unless the necessity drives me." And he hung up.

That strange impulse however, to which in the serious and gay humour that possessed him he had given the name of the necessity, allowed him to wander slowly down the station road, till he saw Richardson walking swiftly along to meet him; then he quickened his own steps. They looked at each other curiously.

"And so", Richardson said at last, "you think that the common things will return?"

"I'm quite certain of it," Anthony said. "Won't He have mercy on all that He's made?"

The other shook his head, and then suddenly smiled. "Well, if you and they like it that way, there's no more to be said," he answered. "Myself, I think you're only wasting time on the images."

"Well, who made the images?" Anthony asked. "You sound like a medieval monk commenting on marriage. Don't be so stuck-up over your old way, whatever it is. What actually is it?"

Richardson pointed to the sky. "Do you see the light of that fire?" he asked. "Yes, there. Berringer's house has been burning all day."

"I know, I saw it."

"I'm going out there," Richardson said and stopped.

"But—I'm not saying you're wrong—but why?" Anthony asked. "Isn't fire an image too?"

"That perhaps," the other answered. "But all this——" he touched his clothes and himself, and his eyes grew dark with a sudden passion of desire—"has to go somehow; and if the fire that will destroy the world is here already, it isn't I that will keep from it."

Anthony looked at him a little ruefully. "I'm sorry," he said. "I'd hoped we might have talked more. And—you know best —but you're quite sure you're right? I can't see but what the images have their place. *Ex umbris* perhaps, but the noon has to drive the shadows away naturally, hasn't it?"

The other shrugged. "O I know," he said. "It's all been argued a hundred times, Jensenist and Jesuit, the monk and the married man, mystic and sacramentalist. But all I know is that I must make for the End when and as soon as I see it. Perhaps that's why I am alone. But since that's so—I'd like you, if you will, and if restoration comes, to give this book back to Berringer if he's alive, and to keep it if he isn't. What," he added, "what you call alive."

The Naming of the Beasts

Anthony took the little parcel. "I will do it," he said. "But I only call it alive because the images must communicate, and communication is such a jolly thing. However, I'm keeping you and I mustn't do that . . . as we sacramentalists say."

They shook hands. Then Anthony broke out again. "I do wish you weren't—No; no, I don't. Go with God."

"Go with God," the other's more sombre voice answered. They stood for a moment, then they stepped apart, their hands went up in mutual courteous farewell, and they went their separate ways.

No-one saw the young bookseller's assistant again; no-one thought of him, except his employer and his landlady, and each of them, grumbling first, afterwards filled his place and forgot him. Alone and unnoticed he went along the country road to his secret end. Only Anthony, as he went swiftly to Damaris, commended the other's soul to the Maker and Destroyer of images.

Damaris herself opened the door to him when he came. She was about to speak when he prevented her by saying happily: "So you found him?" "He's asleep upstairs now,"she answered. "And you?" He pulled her closer to him. "Why, that I'll tell you presently," he said. "Tell me first. How beautifully you seem to do your job!"

"The doctor's here," she said. "I managed to get him round earlier in the day, and he said he'd come again before night. Come and see him."

"Is it Rockbotham?" Anthony asked, moving with her up the stairs. "He's a good creature."

"I used to think he was rather a dull sort of fool," Damaris said. "But to-day he was quite strong and wise. O Anthony"— she checked at the door of the bedroom—"don't hate me, will you?"

"When I hate you," he answered, "the place of the angels will be desolate and our necessity will forget itself."

The Naming of the Beasts

"What is our necessity?" she asked, looking up at him as they passed.

"It's just to be, I suppose," Anthony answered slowly. "I mean, the simpler one is the nearer one is to loving. If the pattern's arranged in me, what can I do but let myself be the pattern? I can see to it that I don't hate, but after that Love must do his own business. But let's go on now, may we? And talk of this another day."

"Tell me just one thing first," Damaris said. "Do you think—I've been wondering this afternoon—do you think it's wrong of me to work at Abelard?"

"Darling, how can intelligence be wrong?" he answered. "I should think you knew more about him than anyone else in the world, and it's a perfectly sound idea to make a beautiful thing of what you know. So long as you don't neglect me in order to do it."

"And is that being impersonal?" she mocked him.

"Why, yes," he said, "for that's your job too. And all your job is impersonal and one. Or personal and one—it doesn't matter which you say. They're only debating words really. Come on, let's go in."

As Anthony looked at Dr. Rockbotham he felt that Damaris was right. The first glance had been for his friend, but Quentin seemed to be sleeping quietly, and the doctor was on the point of coming towards the door. He had never been a particularly notable figure until now, but now indeed, in the hackneyed but convincing phrase, Anthony saw him for the first time. The lines of his face were unaltered, but it was moulded in a great strength and confidence; the eyes were deep and wise; the mouth closed firmly as if on the oath of Hippocrates—the seal of silence and the knowledge of discretion. "Aesculapius," Anthony thought to himself, and remembered the snake that was the symbol of Aesculapius. "We sneer at medicine," he thought, "but after all we *do* know more—not much, but a little. We sneer at progress, but we do, in a way, progress; the gods haven't abandoned man." For a moment he dreamed of a white-robed bearded figure, with a great serpent coiled by him, where in some remote temple of Epidaurus or Pergamus the child of Phoebus Apollo laboured to heal men by the art that he had learned from the two-formed Cheiron, the master of herbs. Zeus had destroyed him by lightning at last, since by his wisdom the dead were recalled to life, and the sacred order of the world was in danger of being broken. But the serpent-wreathed rod was still outstretched and still the servants of the art were sent out by their father on missions of health. He shook hands gravely, as if in ritual.

"I think he'll do very well," the doctor was saying, and the vowels of the simple words came to Anthony's ears heavy with the harmonies of Greek. "Exhaustion—absolute exhaustion: he must have been struck by a kind of panic. But sleep, and quiet, and food, will put him right. The proper kind of food."

"Ah that!" Anthony exclaimed.

"But whether you can manage him here for a day or two," the doctor went on to Damaris, "in the circumstances. He could of course be moved——"

"I don't think there's any need," she answered, and then in answer to Anthony's eyebrows, "My father died this afternoon."

Anthony nodded; it was no more than he had expected.

"There isn't any need to sit up with him," the doctor went on, "and twenty-four hours' entire rest would make a great difference. Still, it's perhaps rather hard on you, Miss Tighe——"

Damaris put out her hand. "Ah, no!" she said. "Certainly he must be here. He is Anthony's friend and mine. I am very, very glad he is here," and her other hand caught Anthony's and with an intense pressure told him all that that sentence meant of restoration and joy.

The Naming of the Beasts

After a little more conversation the doctor went, and Damaris and Anthony looked at each other in the hall.

"I won't say I'm sorry about your father," he said. "I think he had ended his business," and as she smiled in a profound assent, he went on, "and now I must get on with mine."

She looked at him anxiously, but said nothing for a minute, while he waited: then she asked, "You will let me come— wherever it is?"

"Come," he said, and held out his hand, and so without any delay they went out of the front door and along the street together. The town was caught in the terror; the street lay empty before them. A profound stillness was all round them, except that in some house near at hand a baby was wailing. The sound was the only audible sign of humanity; it was humanity. All man's courage and knowledge came to this in the end—Damaris, listening, remembered having read somewhere that the god who had given his name to the building which was the home of the greatest bishop in the world, the centre of the Roman Church, the shrine (it was said) of infallible authority, was Vaticanus, and the office of Vaticanus was to preside over the new-born child's first cry. That was all; that was all that the Vatican itself could do, and all that the Vatican held. Here the spirit of man could but reach that far—and as she pondered it, the thunder crashed out again. What she had called thunder, but it was clearer now; it was the roar of a living creature. She heard it, and heard it answered. At her side Anthony had paused, thrown up his head, and sent out another cry upon the night. It was an incomprehensible call, and it broke out right in the midst of that other reverberating roar and checked and silenced it. It was a sound as of a single word, but not English, nor Latin, nor Greek. Hebrew it might have been or something older than Hebrew, some incantation whereby the prediluvian magicians had controlled contentions among spirits or the language in which our father Adam named the beasts of the garden. The roar ceased on the moment, and then as at Anthony's movement they began again to walk on, there rose about them a little breeze. It was very light, hardly more than a ruffling of the air, but it stirred her hair, and breathed on her face, and even gently shook the light silk sleeves of her frock. She stole a glance at Anthony, and met his eyes. He was smiling and she broke into an answering smile. But it was not until they had gone some way farther that she spoke.

"Where are we going?" she said.

"I think we are going to the field where you found Quentin," he answered. "Do you remember what you saw there?"

She nodded. "And——?" she said, waiting for him to go on. But he did not, only after some minutes he said softly, "It was good of you to look for Quentin."

"Good!" she exclaimed. "Good! O Anthony!"

"Well, so it was," he answered. "Or good in you. How accurate one has to be with one's prepositions! Perhaps it was a preposition wrong that set the whole world awry."

"It was", she said, "a preposition that helped to divide the Church."

"Sweetest of theologians," he answered, "I will make it my chief business always to be accurate in my prepositions about you. It shall be good *in* you always, and good *of* you never."

"Not even for a treat?" she asked.

"O for a treat," he answered, "you shall be the good in itself, the rose-garden of the saints. Will you meet me there to-morrow evening?"

"So soon?" she said. "Will the saints expect me?"

"Image of sanctity," he answered, "they will look in you as a mirror to see the glory of God that is about them, by so much will your soul be clearer than theirs."

"I suppose that's what you mean by a treat," she said. "It sounds to me like several at once."

"But for a treat to me you must believe it," he said, "for as long as it takes your finger to mark the line of life on your hand."

"Supposing I believed it too long?" she said, half-seriously.

"Why, for fear of that," he answered, "you will remember that what is seen in you is present in all, and that the beauty of every other living creature is as bright as yours."

"And that", she said, "sounds like the morning after the party."

"It is the present given at the party," he said, "and perhaps what the party itself was for."

They were out of the town, and coming to the stile where Damaris had been twice with Quentin. The time had seemed very quick, but the happiness that beat in her breast had shortened it, she supposed, or else the wind that, stronger now, seemed to carry them along. By the stile they paused and looked over and down the sloping fields beyond; and Damaris suddenly saw and recollected the great glow in the sky, and away below them the tree of fire that burned in the place of the house. She had entirely forgotten it as she came along the road with Anthony, and now she realized that it was beneath the reflection of that terrible thing that their interchange of laughing truths had gone on. So joyous they had been; so awful were the dangers that surrounded them. Her breath came quicker; she looked at Anthony, and saw his face had changed from tenderness to high authority. He dropped her hand and turned to the stile. For a moment she flinched.

"Ah, must you go?" she cried. She knew somehow that she would not; she must stay there. Less practised than he, immature in doctrine and deed, she has her place on the hither side of the work. He did not seem to hear her; lightly he laid his hand on the stile and vaulted over, and as her eyes followed him she exclaimed again at what she saw. It was almost dark, and the shadows were confusing, for the fire below did not seem to cast a light on the land, but it seemed to her that the land was changed. It fell away very steeply beneath her, in an open glade, round which on either side trees grew; not the trees of English hedges, but mightier and taller growths. She saw palms waving, and other immense things shaken by the strength of the swiftly rising wind. Huge and shining leaves were tossed in the air; the high grass of the dark glade itself was swept this way and that by the same energy. The glade ran right down to the bottom of the steep descent, and there in its centre was the fire that surged in the shape of a tree—no, it *was* a tree, one of two that grew there, side by side, and otherwise alone. The one at which she had been gazing was still vivid with fiery colour; by it grew a dark mass in which no tone or hint of colour showed. Far above the ground the boughs and foliage interlaced, golden light and heavy blackness were intermingled. But while she looked, the figure of Anthony came between her and the trees, if indeed it were still Anthony, and yet she knew it was. But he was different; he seemed gigantic in the uncertain light, and he was passing with huge strides down the glade. As he moved it seemed to her that he was wearing not clothes but skins, as in some old picture Adam might have fared forth from Paradise. He went on till he was about half-way down the glade, and then he stood still. About him the wind had become a terrific storm; it soared and rushed through the great trees on either hand, yet over it she heard his voice crying. He had stood still, and turned a little, and upon one mighty shoulder there perched a huge bird—at least, it seemed like a bird and, as he called it spread its wings and again closed them. She dimly remembered some other similar motion, and suddenly recaptured it—so the loathsome thing of her own experience had perched outside the windows of her mind, so it had threatened and almost beaten down her life. From such a bestial knowledge she had been barely saved; with a full pulse of gratitude she offered herself, in her own small place, to divine Wisdom.

Anthony—Adam—whatever giant stood before her between the trees of an aboriginal forest—was calling as he had called in the streets of the town. But now he uttered not one word but many, pausing between each, and again giving to each the same strong summons. He called and he commanded; nature lay expectant about him. She was aware then that the forest all round was in movement; living creatures showed themselves on its edge, or hurried through the grass. At each word that he cried, new life gathered, and still the litany of invocation and command went on. By the names that were the Ideas he called them, and the Ideas who are the Principles of everlasting creation heard him, the Principles of everlasting creation who are the Cherubim and Seraphim of the Eternal. In their animal manifestations, duly obedient to the single animal who was lord of the animals, they came. She saw the horse pushing its head over his shoulder; she saw the serpent rearing itself and lightly coiling round his body. Only, but now motionless, the eagle sat on his shoulder, observant of all things, as philosophical knowledge studies the natures and activities of men.

They were returning, summoned by the authority of man from their incursion into the world of man. She thought of the town behind her from which the terror was now withdrawing; she thought of the world which had not known what was approaching and now might sleep on in peace. She thought of Quentin and of her father, the one rescued from his fear, the other absorbed by his content. And as she thought, crouched by the stile that seemed as if it were the way into the Garden, only unguarded for this single night by the fire which was its central heart—as she crouched and thought, she wondered with a sharp pain if he who had gone from her was ever to return. Was she to lose that others might gain? was she to be deprived of her lover that Quentin Sabot might be saved from madness? Where anyhow was Anthony? what was this nightmare in which she was held? Out of a sepulchre of death the old Damaris rushed up into the new; anger began to swell within her. Either this was all a horrid dream or else Anthony had lured her into some insane midnight expedition. It was always the same—no-one ever considered her; no-one thought about her. Her father had died at a most inconvenient moment; there would be all the business of what small capital he had. No-one, no-one, ever considered her, and the work she was trying unselfishly to do as a contribution to the history of philosophical thought.

Something, however, still held. As, in the renewed and full pseudo-realization of what she was and what she was doing by her work—hers, hers, the darling hers!—she moved to rise (even in a nightmare she needn't crouch), something for one second held her down. It held her—that slender ligature of unrealized devotion—for the second that the old hateful thing took to flood her and a little to recede. The years of selfish toil had had at any rate this good—they had been years of toil; she had not easily abandoned any search because of difficulty, and that habit of intention, by its own power of good, offered her salvation then. The full flood receded; she remembered herself, and her young soul struggled to reach the bright shore beyond the gloomy waters that tossed it. The thing that was the opposite of the pterodactyl, the thing that had been the purpose of the search of Abelard, the thing that was Anthony and yet wasn't Anthony—that. She knew it; as she did so she felt her own name called, and cried out in agony "Yes, yes." If Anthony must go, then he must go. He—it—knew; she didn't. Her limbs were released; she sprang up, the older energies renewed almost to fierceness in her determination to discover that other thing. She would be savage with herself, royal in daring, a lioness in hunger and in the hunt. Of that thing itself, she knew little but that it was blessed, innocent and joyous; it was a marvel of white knowledge, as much of earth as any tender creature of the fields, yet bound to its heavenly origin by hypostatic union of experience. A fierce conquest, an innocent obedience—these were to be her signs.

The sound of her name still echoed through her spirit when, recovered from her inner struggle, she looked again upon the glade of the garden where the image of Adam named the beasts, and naming ruled them. But now he was farther from her, nearer to those twin mysterious trees in the centre. Among the shapes that pressed about him she could not at first well discern one from another, but as she leaned and strained to see she beheld them gathering into two companies. There fell over the whole scene a strange and lovely clearness, shed from the wings of a soaring wonder that left the shoulder where it had reposed and flew, scattering light. The intermingled foliage of the trees of knowledge and of life—if indeed they were separate—received it; amid those branches the eagle which was the living act of science sank and rested. But far below the human figure stood and on either side of it were the shapes of the lion and the lamb. His hand rested on the head of the one; the other paused by him. In and for that exalted moment all acts of peace that then had being through the world were deepened and knew their own nature more clearly; away in villages and towns such spirits as the country doctor in Smetham received a measure of content in their work. Friendships grew closer; intentions of love possessed their right fulfilment. Terrors of malice and envy and jealousy faded; disordered beauty everywhere recognized again the sacred laws that governed it. Man dreamed of himself in the place of his creation.

The vision passed from them, and from the woman who watched as Eve might have watched the movements of her companion. He looked on the beasts and seemed to speak to them, and slowly they withdrew. Slowly, each after its own habit, they moved along the glade, and suddenly the lamb was lost to her sight under the massed heaviness of those trees from which they had come. On the very edge of the mystery the lion looked back, half turned towards the way it had gone. Its eyes met those of the man who faced it, but he came no farther. His just concern was still with the world of men and women, and with his gaze he bade the angelical pass back and close the breach. It broke into one final roar—the woman heard and

trembled, and heard the roar cease as the Adam answered and
quelled it with the sound of its own name. She saw it turn
again and move away, and on the very instant the human
figure itself turned and at full speed ran towards her. The
earth shook under her; from the place of the trees there broke
again the pillar of flame, as if between the sky and earth a fiery
sword were shaken, itself "with dreadful faces thronged and
fiery arms." The guard that protected earth was set again; the
interposition of the Mercy veiled the destroying energies from
the weakness of men.

One of the firemen who, late at night, and ignorant of the
aspect under which Damaris from the ridge beheld that super-
naturally deepened valley, still attempted to subdue the fire
which raged in the house, said afterwards, when his wife spoke
to him of the wild rumours that had till midnight possessed the
town, that he also had thought that he saw, as he faced the
ridge, a great shape of a lion leap from the field straight into the
flames. It was directly afterwards that their prolonged efforts
were unexpectedly successful; the fire dwindled, sank, and in a
short time expired. It was the same man who had thought that,
earlier in the evening, he had seen a young man slip past his
comrades towards the pyre, but since he had seen no more of
him he concluded it could not have been so. The house itself,
and the bodies of the owner and the housekeeper, had been
reduced to the finest ash; there was, when the fire died out,
nothing but a layer of ash spread over the earth. It was, in
short, one of the worst fires he had ever known, and the heat
and blaze had at moments evidently dazed him.

But Damaris, when from the glade that behind him became
once more nothing but the English fields she received the
flying figure of Anthony, did not think she had been dazed. He
leapt the stile, stretching out his hand to her as she came, and
she caught it, and was swung across the road before he could
stop himself. Panting from his rush he smiled at her; panting

from her intense vigil she breathed all herself back. Then their hands fell apart, and after a little they began to walk slowly on.

In a minute he looked at her. "I say, you're not cold, are you?" he asked. "I wish you'd got a coat or something."

"It's not very far," she answered. "No, I'm not cold."